ON THE WALL

Anne Fine

Old Barn Books

ON THE WALL

For Teddy

First published in the UK in 2024 by
Old Barn Books Ltd
West Sussex
RH20 2JW

Old Barn Books Ltd is an independent
UK-based publisher of picture books and fiction
Teaching resources for our books are available to download from our website.
www.oldbarnbooks.com

Follow us on Facebook, X or Instagram: @oldbarnbooks

We are proud to be distributed in the UK by Bounce Sales & Marketing Ltd
www.bouncemarketing.co.uk

Editorial consultant: Jake Hope
Cover illustration © 2024 Keaton Henson

9781910646991
eBook ISBN 9781910646502

1 3 5 7 9 10 8 6 4 2

Here We Go Again

Finley Edward Tandy was sitting at the bottom of the stairs, tying the laces on his new black school shoes.

"Get a move on," his brother Luke said, "or I won't have time to go with you as far as the gates."

"How long was I at my last school?" Finley asked his mother. She was in the doorway, waiting to see him off on this, his first morning, before she left for work.

She tipped her head to think. "Well, not counting your year in nursery, it was seven years."

"Seven whole years!" He seemed amazed at the thought. "That is an awfully long time."

"Good thing you did something useful, then," his brother said, "and learned to read and write."

"And count," said Finley. He turned back to his

mother. "So how long will I be at this school?"

"If you last to the very end," teased Luke.

"If I last to the very end."

This time his mother had already worked it out. "Another seven."

"Another seven!" If possible, Finley seemed even more astonished. He turned to Luke. "Did you do *fourteen whole years* in school before you left?"

"I must have," Luke said, somewhat surprised himself. "Now hurry up!"

Finley tightened the laces on the second shoe and stood up. He hugged his mother and reached for his sturdy new school bag stamped with the Windfields School crest.

"Right, then," he told her cheerfully. "Here we go again."

Some Hopes

Juliet's father walked her all the way to the school gates. She held his hand tightly until she spotted others in the same uniform who were going the same way. Then she pulled away.

"You'll be all right," he tried to reassure her. "Truly you will. Just try and remember what Surina taught you, and breathe out slowly and gently whenever you get to feel tense."

She didn't say a word, so he suggested yet again, "Or I can come in with you, and explain."

"No!" Juliet said fiercely. "I'll be all right. I want to try this by myself. I don't want people feeling sorry for me."

Her father laid his hands on her shoulders and

turned her to face him. "Look," he said, "Mum being so ill for so long was *horrible*. For both of us, Nobody was surprised you went to pieces afterwards. But think how much better you were feeling even last year. Miles better. You managed to get to school and stay there most of almost every day. And this year might turn out to be even easier. Fresh start, and all that."

He reached for Juliet's hand just long enough to squeeze it, and they turned to walk on. Now they were nearing the entrance to Windfields School, the pavements were much busier, with others slowing their progress by gathering in untidy groups, or pushing past, shouting to friends.

"They're all so *big*," breathed Juliet.

"Not all of them. The ones in your class will be mostly the same as you." He pointed. "See. There are Cherry and Jamie, just ahead."

Juliet craned to see them, and for the first time in her life wished that she, too, was a twin. She would feel safer.

At that moment, Cherry turned.

"You have to go now," Juliet told her dad, panicking. "Nobody else's parents are going through the gates."

He hesitated before saying, "Bye, then, sweetheart. Try to have good time."

Some hopes, thought Juliet. But she couldn't bring herself to say it aloud in case he worried about her even more. She couldn't have stood that.

Into Battle

Mr Goodhew drove into the first free space he could find in Windfields School's new staff car park, and slid his permit onto the dashboard so that the name printed on it could be clearly seen.

Julian Goodhew.

"Right, then," he told himself cheerfully. "Here we go again. Into battle."

Autumn Term

Nothing special

Mr Goodhew left one or two of the heavier boxes in the back of the car and went straight to his home room to meet his brand-new class. As usual, a lot of their blazers hung a little too long. ("Room for growth," as the parents probably muttered, paying for all the items of uniform and sports gear their offspring were going to need.) And, as he did at the start of every school year, Mr Goodhew took a few moments to look around the room and try to guess which of the young people staring back at him might turn out to be a bit of a problem – too cheeky? too sullen? maybe a bit too talkative? His eyes rested on Finley Tandy for barely a moment. The boy looked no more nervous or uncomfortable than any of the others. He wasn't fidgeting, or making silly faces at old friends from his primary school. He wasn't whispering, or sniggering, or looking as if, at the first opportunity, he might step out of line.

No. Nothing special about that boy in the third row. Nothing at all.

The full Finley you shall be

It was nearly an hour later before Mr Goodhew had his first moments of doubt about Finley. He had been calling them up to his desk, one by one, to have a quick private chat, and he was well over halfway down the register.

"Finley Tandy," he called out, and waited for the boy to come up beside him before laying a finger on the printed list in front of him. "Right, then. I have your first names down as Finley Edward. So all I need to know right now is if you're happy with the name Finley."

The boy stared blankly. "Happy with it?"

"Yes. I'm just checking. I mean, are you all right with being called Finley by all your teachers? Or do you prefer to use Edward? Or maybe even something else. Finn, maybe?"

"Finn?"

"Yes," Mr Goodhew said patiently. "I've had three Finleys through my classes in my time, and two of them turned out to be Finns."

Since the boy still looked mystified, Mr Goodhew explained. "A lot of you come to us with one name on your paperwork, but another you actually use." He added a couple of examples. "Like most Benjamins are Ben, and one or two of our Mohammeds are always called Mo. I'm simply asking you what name you prefer to use."

"But I don't use my name," said Finley Tandy. "It's only other people who ever have to say it."

Mr Goodhew inspected the boy's face. Was he trying to be clever? He could be a little bit slow on the uptake, of course. Or he could be one of those pupils who truly do see the world in a purely literal fashion? Whatever it was, Mr Goodhew decided that this was a busy morning, and he didn't have time to worry about it. "Right, then," he said. "Since you don't have a problem, the full Finley you shall be."

He marked the name typed on the list with a small tick, and finished off with the short speech he made to every one of them when, for the first time, he was speaking to them privately like this. "Now, Finley, I want you to be sure to come to me with any problems you may have. Anything at all. And I hope you'll be really happy in this school."

"Oh, I'll be happy," Finley said. "I'm happy absolutely everywhere. And all the time."

And he went back to his desk.

All right?

As soon as the second buzzer sounded, everyone went off for lessons. So the next time that Mr Goodhew spotted Finley it was almost at the end of break. He was sitting, idly swinging his legs, on the flat-topped wall that ran between the recreation ground and the now abandoned old school car park behind. On an impulse, as Mr Goodhew walked past, he stopped for a moment to ask the boy, "All right?"

"Yes, thank you," Finley answered politely.

Mr Goodhew glanced round. With no one else within earshot, he felt free to ask, "Do you know any of the others? There must be one or two, at least, who've come up from the same primary school as you."

"Eight of them," Finley told him. He reeled off their names. "Jamie and Cherry, Alicia, Akeem, Maria, Jia Li, Stuart and Katherine."

"But you're not spending break time with any of them?"

"No."

"Is there a reason for that?"

The boy shrugged. "Not really, no."

Mr Goodhew wasn't convinced, but he remembered what Finley had told him earlier that morning. "Well," he said heartily, "you did tell me you were happy all the time."

"Yes," Finley said. "And I think I'm probably very good indeed at being happy by myself."

Red dots on a map

Mr Goodhew wasn't the only one to have noticed Finley on the wall by himself. Mrs Harris, who taught everyone Geography, prided herself on her ability to notice those of the newcomers who might be finding it difficult to settle in. In the first lesson she'd had with them that morning, she'd handed to each of them a rather faded photocopied map of the world. Mrs Harris had been teaching this first 'getting-to-know-you' lesson for so many years that one or two of the countries on the map were labelled with names they had long since forsaken, and some of the national borders had shifted quite a lot. But since the only thing she wanted her pupils to do was think about their friends and family, and put red dots on their map to indicate where these lived, that scarcely mattered.

"Some of you," she assured them before they began, "will find that a lot of your dots are all on top of one another because most of your family and friends live very near you, around here. And one or two of you – " – and here Mrs Harris put on a specially comforting look, and used her most sympathetic tone of voice – " – will find your dots are more spread out over the map."

You could learn quite a lot about them, she'd found, just from the questions they asked her while they were doing this first task.

"Do they have to be *real* friends?"

"What if their family had to leave Sudan right after yours did, but you're not yet sure where they ended up?"

"Do online friends count? What if you don't know

exactly where they live?"

"Can I count someone I met on holiday and really, really liked, but I'm not sure would even remember me, because it was so long ago?"

And the saddest of all: "What if you can't think of anybody at all?"

Mrs Harris drifted around the room until she reached Finley. Since he was the boy she'd noticed sitting on a wall all by himself for fully twenty minutes, speaking to no one, she made a point of looking to see where he'd put red dots on his map. And, truly, it might as well have had measles. They were all over the British Isles. There were several in various parts of Asia, at least five in the United States, and quite a few in Italy and Spain.

"These are all friends and family?"

"Yes," Finley told her confidently.

"You've certainly got a lot of them."

"I do."

"That's nice," said Mrs Harris and went back to her desk, wondering if the boy was inventing a life knee deep in friends and family he didn't have, or whether, when she was fretting that he might be a bit of a loner, she'd got him totally, totally wrong.

A bit of a strange one

As he walked out of the lunch hall, Mr Goodhew spotted Finley back on the wall. He was alone again, but cross-legged this time. Mr Goodhew wondered for a moment if he should stop to exchange a few more words with the boy, then decided he'd rather go on to the staffoom. But Finley stayed in his mind, and, pouring scalding water over his tea bag a couple of minutes later, he told the other teachers who were gathered there: "That Finley Tandy I've landed is a bit of a strange one."

"They're all strange," Dr Yates said. She stretched out a foot to press open the pedal bin so Mr Goodhew could drop his tea bag inside. "My theory is that, if you don't think they're strange, it's just because you don't yet know them."

"Well, this one's *different* strange," insisted Mr Goodhew. "Out of a completely new box."

"In what way?"

Mr Goodhew wondered how best to put it. His sister had been a yoga teacher for a while, and in the end he said, "I suppose I think he's what a meditation expert might describe as 'centred'."

Dr Rutter, who taught Chemistry, was clearly baffled. "Centred?"

"Well, put it this way. He's peculiarly calm."

Dr Yates said, "I only wish we had a few more like that. In fact, I could do with a whole class of them. What did you say his name was?"

"Finley. Finley Tandy."

"Have we had other Tandys?"

Everyone looked towards Mrs Harris, who was reckoned to be the best at remembering past pupils. Scraping a few last, unwanted strands of her lunch time noodles into the bin, she said, "We had a Luke Tandy, but he must have left at least three years ago. If this one is his brother, that is quite a gap."

"Where did this Finley come up from?" Mr Brownlow asked.

Mr Goodhew did a brain search for a few of the

names Finley had mentioned. "The same as a Cherry, and an Akeem and an Alicia."

"Janson Road Primary, then," said Mrs Harris.

Mr Brownlow snorted. "This Finley won't have learned his meditative skills in Janson Road Primary, that's for sure!"

"Maybe he was taught them in order to survive the place," Dr Yates suggested.

The buzzer sounded for the start of afternoon school. Glancing out of the window, Mr Goodhew saw Finley Tandy slide off the wall and walk towards the south doors. Several of the younger boys going in the same direction slowed as he came close and, almost imperceptibly, Finley appeared to be accepted into the group. One of them even put an arm round Finley's shoulders in a friendly fashion.

So, Mr Goodhew thought, no obvious ill-feeling there. He can't have been on that wall to try to stay away from them. He hadn't *needed* to keep apart from all the noisy chaos of the lunch hour break.

He'd clearly simply been preferring to spend his time that way.

Not an exam

Mr Goodhew took the class himself early that first afternoon. He handed out copies of the test that Dr Yates gave to all the new pupils so she could see which maths set they would fit into best. Dr Yates always insisted that the test was taken in silence, and so, to make that easier to enforce, Mr Goodhew asked all of them to shunt their desks apart.

He knew the test of old. It started with the easiest possible questions, and gradually became harder and harder. He told the class, "Now don't expect to finish. Nobody finishes, so you mustn't get discouraged, or panic. Just work your way through steadily and calmly, as far as you can. Try not to get bogged down. If you can't do one of the questions, move on to the next and try that. You only stop when you're quite sure you can't do any more at all." Seeing the boy called Stuart seemed already to be close to tears, Mr Goodhew took a moment more to tell them firmly, "This is *not* an exam. We don't give marks for it. It's more for us than for you. It's just the simplest way to help us work out which maths group will suit you best for now."

He watched as they picked up their pens and pencils and began to grind their way through the questions Dr Yates had designed for them. Some started very quickly. Others looked as if they might be toiling badly even on the first page. Katherine was clearly racing along with no trouble.

The girl called Juliet still just sat there looking terrified.

Shoulders down. Breathe out. Slowly, slowly.

Juliet could actually feel her knees knocking against one another under the desk. It wasn't that she was *bad* at maths. Juliet knew that. She knew that, safe at home with her dad, she'd always got the work done. It was just that it was a test. Mr Goodhew might try to tell them that it wasn't an exam, but really it was, of course. If it was testing something, then it was a test.

And Juliet knew it didn't matter anyway. Hadn't her dad said often enough, "No test on earth is that important, Juliet. Everyone just wants you to be happy. Just try your hardest, and that's the best that you can do,

and that will always, *always*, be good enough for me."
(She couldn't remember her mum ever saying anything
at all about tests. But then again, before her mum got
ill, Juliet had never seemed to have any tests at all – or
maybe she'd not even noticed them.)

Juliet stared at the paper on which the little black
marks seemed to be dancing. She did what Surina had
taught her, and what they still practised together every
single session. She shut her eyes and took a deep, deep
breath. She dropped her shoulders as low as they would
go, and let the breath out again, slowly, slowly, slowly.

Then she opened her eyes. The marks on the paper
gradually turned back into numbers and words and
figures. She could read them now.

Juliet picked up her pen and began.

"I was just looking at the little marks."

From time to time, Mr Goodhew ambled around the
classroom, curious to see how they were doing. He mostly
taught physics himself, and he had found over the years
that, as they grew older, many of the ones who shone at

maths ended up keeping on with his subject as well. He wandered up and down between the desks, watching as more and more of them slowed up, or crossed out things they'd clearly only just written. Some raised their heads more often. One or two sighed heavily.

As they laid down their pens and pencils, Mr Goodhew strolled up to them. "Finished? Do you want to look through again, or just give me your paper now?"

Most of them handed over their papers with relief. Towards the end, only Katherine and Jia Li were still working busily. Finley, Mr Goodhew noticed, had turned back to the very first page of easy questions, and was staring down at it.

"You mustn't *worry*," Mr Goodhew assured him quietly. "It really isn't an exam."

"No," Finley whispered back. "I was just looking at the little marks."

"Little marks?"

"You know." And Finley pointed, first to a plus and then to a multiplication sign.

"Oh," Mr Goodhew said. "You mean the mathematical *symbols*."

"Yes," Finley answered. "I was thinking about how neat they are."

Mr Goodhew decided it was time for a joke "Well," he said dryly, "that will depend a very great deal on who is writing them."

"I didn't mean *that* sort of neat," explained Finley. "I meant that they don't need much to let you know what they mean."

The buzzer sounded. Mr Goodhew raised his voice to speak to the rest of the class. "That's it. Everyone can go off to their next lesson now. Just leave your papers on your desk. Katherine and Jia Li, I know you'd quite like to carry on, but I'm not sure there's any need for it now you've already shown what you can do."

Katherine appeared to not even have heard him, but Jia Li obediently put the cap on her pen and left along with the others. Mr Goodhew turned back to Finley, who was still studying his very first page.

"I mean they're so *simple*," Finley said admiringly. He pointed. "Look at the take away thing."

"The minus sign," said Mr Goodhew automatically.

Finley ignored the correction. "Yes. I mean, it's just

a tiny line. Just one tiny line you can write in no time at all." He used his finger to point, first to a plus, then to a multiplication sign. "And look at these two. They're exactly the same, but one's just tipped over a bit." He ran his finger along the line again. "And this one."

"The division sign."

"Yes. Just a minus with two tiny added dots! I mean, whoever thought of that? It's brilliant! They're so – " He looked up. "Well, what *is* the word, if it's not 'neat'?"

"Economical," said Mr Goodhew, "in the sense of no effort wasted."

"Yes, that's it!" Finley's face was radiant. "I mean, they're so unbelievably clever! Who was it thought of them?"

Mr Goodhew was flummoxed, but he did his best. "I'm afraid I don't know. I'm pretty sure the plus sign was the first. And that must have been at least seven hundred years ago. But as for the rest, I'd have to look it up."

Finley was staring into space. "Seven hundred years! That is *amazing*. People weren't stupid back then, were they? They *can't* have been, if they could think of something as absolutely clever and simple as that."

Just then, Katherine came up to them, brandishing her paper with a triumphant smile. "I'm finished now." Handing what she had done to Mr Goodhew, she rushed towards the door. Mr Goodhew took the chance to reach out for Finley's paper as well. "Right, then," he told him. "Off you go."

He watched as Finley walked out, then shook his head. And it was obvious from the look on Mr Goodhew's face that he was thinking, "Strange boy. Not at all stupid, then. But yes, a strange one . . . "

I can be quiet anywhere

The last teacher to have Finley Tandy in her room on that first day was Ms Fuentes. She'd shown her new class a short film about Spain, and introduced them to the Spanish names for some of their favourite foods. The buzzer sounded and she let them go. The room cleared quickly, and as the clattering and the foot falls died down, Ms Fuentes began stuffing books and papers into her bag.

When she looked up, there was one boy still sitting in his place. He looked neither happy nor sad. He just looked like himself.

She nearly said, "Not got a home to go to?" But some of them, of course, came from the sorts of families where no child in their senses would be keen to hurry back. Instead, she asked, "Are you okay there?"

He nodded. "I'm fine."

Discreetly, Ms Fuentes opened her desk drawer a few inches, so she could see the plan she'd drawn up right at the start of the lesson, when she'd asked each of them to say their name. ("*¿Como te llamas?*") It was a useful guide until she knew them better.

"It's Finley, isn't it?"

"That's right."

He just sat tight.

"No problem, then? Nothing you wanted to ask me?"

He shook his head. "No, thank you. I was just sitting here, being quiet."

"The problem is," she said, "that I'm not allowed to leave the room till you're all gone. So..."

"Oh, okay," he told her cheerfully. "I don't mind leaving now. I can be quiet anywhere. Really."

And, scooping up his school bag, off he went, into

the noisy going-home chaos of the corridor.

Ms Fuentes followed Finley to the doorway, and watched as he threaded his way serenely through the milling hordes.

'Odd child', she couldn't help but think. But then, just as he reached the double doors at the very end of the corridor, she found herself wondering, "Now why on earth do I think that?"

And, for the life of her, she couldn't think of any passable reason.

We could do with a few more of those

He'd said he could be quiet anywhere and it was true, it seemed. Even before the end of that first week of term, Mr Porter had come across Finley Tandy being quiet in the science lab, well after the lesson had ended. Miss Ellerman found him calmly doing nothing at the back of the gym changing rooms. Mr Harley, the caretaker, had found him, as he put it, 'nesting among the mops' in a store cupboard.

"Could he be from a Quaker family?" asked Mrs

Hilliard. "Quakers are well known for having quiet moments and sitting comfortably in peace."

"He's certainly very good at it," said Mr Goodhew. "And yet he never seems to mind being interrupted."

"How does he get on with the others?" asked Ms Leroy, who hadn't come across the boy yet, though she'd heard a very great deal about him over the last few days.

"That's the odd thing," said Mr Goodhew. "He gets on fine with them. I've seen him swapping yoghurts with other people. I've seen him chatting. I've even seen him being invited into the lunch line, and no one behind complaining."

"Maybe we should simply think of him as nicely well-rounded, then," said Mrs Hilliard. "Balanced. And be grateful his parents picked our school to send him to, and not some other."

Rainbows. Sunshine. Clouds. Light. Gravity.

Some of the class were less taken than Mrs Hilliard with the idea of Finley simply being 'well-rounded'. Only a short while later, finding Finley sitting quietly on the wall, Jeremy asked him, "Why are you so weird?"

"Weird?" Finley smiled. "I don't think that I'm weird."

"I think you are. I know you're not at all shy. You put your hand up and answer questions in class. So just sitting on this wall, not doing anything and not talking to anyone for hours and hours is weird."

"It isn't for hours and hours," Finley argued. "We're not even at the end of break yet, and break is only twenty minutes. And I've just been talking to you." He gazed around calmly. "In any case," he added, "what's weird about wanting to be quiet?"

Jeremy searched for the best way of putting it. "It isn't just being quiet, like Juliet, or Jia Li, or Anthony. It's more like you're being *still*. Or *silent*. Not doing anything except just *being there*. It isn't *natural*."

"You're wrong there," Finley told him. "Lots of silent things are perfectly natural."

"Like what?"

Finley considered. "Well, rainbows, for one," he said. "And sunshine." He thought some more. "Clouds. Light. Gravity."

"They're *different*," Jeremy insisted. "They're not at all

34

like you."

Finley appeared not even to be listening. He was still listing off the things that he could think of that were both natural and silent. "The moon. Plants."

"Stop it!" said Jeremy. "Just stop it!" But by now he was so beside himself with frustration that he was glad the buzzer rang, and he could mutter under his breath, "Well, *I* still think you're weird," and run off into the line that was lengthening at the south door.

No proper friends

Juliet was sitting alone on the bench under the staffroom window. She had no proper friends, and was too shy to hang around any of the other groups until they either let her in or made it clear that she should go away. At her old school there had been what the teachers called a Friendship Bench. You were supposed to sit there if you felt sad or lonely, and people were told in Assembly that it would be nice of them to come and talk to you, or maybe even invite you to play. That worked when you were in the youngest classes. If you got tired of walking

round and round the playground alone, pretending
not to mind, and ended up forcing yourself to be brave
enough to sit on the bench, one of the older children
would usually come over almost at once to befriend you.
Sometimes they would just chat to you until the bell
rang. One or two of the bossier ones might try to force
other people to let you into their game. But you weren't
really welcome if that happened. And if Juliet saw one of
those bossy ones heading in her direction, she'd usually
leaned over to pretend she was just there to tighten the
laces on her trainers before taking off again.

But that was way back then. No one in this school
had yet said anything about this particular seat. But
Juliet suspected that, here, the very idea of a Friendship
Bench would be thought of as something they'd all
left behind in primary school. Perhaps the bench was
really for the teachers. But she'd seen other children
sitting on it with their friends. No one had acted as if
they shouldn't be there. And now, fed up with walking
round and round, trying to look as if she was headed
somewhere, or planning to meet someone else as soon as
they came out from lunch, Juliet just sat down.

That was where Finley joined her. She didn't know him – just that his name was Finley and he was in her class. He had been sitting peaceably on the wall opposite till some of the older boys began booting a ball hard at his legs to make it clear they wanted him to move so they could practise goal shots.

So he'd slid off the wall and walked over. Juliet was sitting at one end of the bench. He parked himself in the middle. She knew if any other boy had wanted to take a break on the bench, and yet not talk to her, he would have sat right at the other end.

But Finley sat in the middle – in fact, even a tiny bit more on her side than on the other.

He clearly didn't think it was a Friendship Bench because he didn't speak to her. Nor did he lean down to pretend he was there to retie his laces. He did keep looking out over the recreation area, but didn't seem to be watching anyone in particular, not even the boys who had displaced him. He was just sitting there, a short way along.

If anyone is looking, Juliet thought, they'll probably assume we know each other. They might even think we're friends, because, if not, he would have made sure to sit right at the other end. I bet we look quite comfortable together. Almost side by side. That tight feeling that she'd had in her stomach every break time so far in this new school loosened a bit. She even seemed to breathe more easily, the way Surina at the clinic had tried to teach her. "Just breathe out, Juliet. And do it slowly, slowly. Drop your tight shoulders downwards. Feel your body relax."

Funny. He hadn't said a single word to her. But when the buzzer rang, a few minutes later, Juliet realised that it had been fine, sitting alongside Finley. Rather like she imagined it would be if she were sitting quietly with a friend.

Pandemonium

Mr Brownlow could hear the pandemonium from all the way along the corridor. It sounded as if a thousand angry prisoners were kicking off a riot in a small cupboard. But it was only his Maths class, mucking about till he came in, one or two minutes late.

Sighing, he pushed open the door. Very few of them were in their seats, and those who were seemed to be bellowing at friends across the room. Two of the girls were arguing loudly with a third, who was trying to plait Simon Parson's overlong hair while he screeched from the pain. Akeem appeared to be banging his head on his desk top, to no apparent purpose. Tory and Katherine were having a fencing match with rulers, shouting "Touché!" over and over.

Only one of the class was sitting in silence. It was Finley Tandy. He appeared to be entirely oblivious to the waves of noise assailing him from all sides. His arms were loosely folded and he was expressionless, facing the window but not even seeming to be looking through it.

As soon as the class spotted Mr Brownlow coming in, the noise died down and everyone who was away from a seat moved hastily back to his or her own place. But Finley didn't turn. He didn't even seem to notice that the commotion round him had come to such a swift end.

How does he *do* it? Mr Brownlow asked himself as he walked over to the board to start the lesson. The boy is entirely wrapped in his own private blanket of silence. How does he *do* it? I would love to learn that trick.

Out of a different box

"It was a *wall* of noise," Mr Brownlow told all the other teachers in the staffroom, and not for the first time, during the following break. "I can't have been more than a minute and a half late at the most, and it was *pandemonium*. I simply cannot describe it."

"You don't need to describe it," Dr Yates told him tartly. "This is a school. We pretty well live through it."

"They create uproar deliberately," said Mr Porter. "They're happier with it. I reckon they make all this noise so they can hide behind it. I think a lot of them are actually *scared* of being quiet. That's why we're forever having to tell them to turn things off or turn things down or take things out of their ears. They are allergic to peace and quiet. They are all terrified of silence, and of the self-reflection it can bring."

"But not this Tandy boy," said Mr Goodhew. "He's out of a different box. As far as I can tell, he would be happy being silent most of the time. He acts as if silence is *precious* to him."

"It would be precious to me," said Mr Porter bitterly, thinking of his two tiny daughters at home, "if I had half the chance of ever getting any of it."

Soothing. Very calm.

Ben was the class clown. Bored during lunch break, he spotted Finley sitting cross legged on the wall, and led his followers across. While they stood waiting for whatever show was about to start, Ben hoisted himself up beside Finley, who turned his head for a moment as if to acknowledge Ben's arrival, but didn't say a word.

Ben crossed his legs in exactly the same way as Finley. He put his hands on the wall in exactly the same way as Finley. He looked in the same direction as Finley, but with a beatific smile spread over his face.

"That isn't right," said Tansy. "Finley doesn't look silly like that."

Rather than tone it down, Ben made his face look even more enraptured.

41

"No, no," persisted Tansy. "You've got the face completely wrong. Finley doesn't do anything except look *normal*. You're grinning like an idiot."

Another of Ben's followers agreed. "Yes. You look a bit like a drunk angel."

"What my Nana calls 'gormless'," explained Tansy. "But Finley is just looking like himself."

Ben dropped the mesmerized expression and tried to look just like himself.

"That's better," Tansy said.

The other followers agreed. "Yes, that's much better."

Ben sat there right through till the end of break, copying Finley doing nothing. There wasn't much to watch, so after a while his acolytes got bored enough to drift away in ones and twos. The minutes passed and then the buzzer sounded. Finley slid off the wall and Ben did the same. Together they walked across to join the line forming outside the south door.

As they went in for afternoon registration, Tansy asked Ben, "Weren't you a bit bored, sitting there with Finley, doing nothing all that time?"

Ben thought about it. "Not really, no," he said. "I

think I rather liked it. It was very soothing. I felt very calm."

Juliet, who was behind them, heard what he said and thought back to when she herself had sat on the bench beside Finley through lunch break. She remembered the feeling she'd had, and yes, Ben was exactly right in the way he described it. It had been very soothing. Very calm.

Enough!

Miss Clements brought the palm of her hand down sharply on the desk. "That is *enough*!"

The class fell silent. Half of them looked at her, astonished, and the rest looked mystified.

"I've had enough!" she repeated. "What is the *matter* with you all today? You're driving me to distraction. Most of you are paying no attention at all. Emma keeps dropping pencils on the floor. Ygor is reading under the desk." She wagged a finger at his startled face. "Oh, yes, Ygor! Don't assume I'm a halfwit. Don't think I haven't spotted what you're doing!" She turned her attention to the other side of the room. "Terence

43

and Jamie seem to be doing nothing except watching that seagull out there trying to get in the wheelie bins. Jia Li can't stop doodling on the cover of her book." She rolled her eyes to heaven. "I'm actually trying to teach you something important. Why can't you behave yourselves? Why can't you all be a bit more like Finley, and *behave*?"

Ygor objected to that. "That isn't fair, Miss Clements. Finley isn't behaving. Finley's just *like* that. He just sits there, not even fidgeting. It's what he *does*."

"That's utter nonsense," said Miss Clements. "If Finley can sit at his desk, not fidgeting, then so can everybody else in this class."

They all pitched in to argue.

"It's easy for Finley. Finley can just do it. He does it all the time."

"He does it even when he doesn't need to do it."

"He was just born that way."

"We can't all be like Finley."

"I don't think I will *ever* be like Finley."

"Finley's *lucky*."

"Yes. Ask his mother. She'll probably say that, even

44

when he was a baby, Finley sat quietly in his stroller, not even yelling."

That is the moment Finley spoke up. "I do wish you'd all stop talking about me as if I were dead or unconscious," he scolded them. "I hope you know that I am sitting here. With two ears that *work*."

Some of them grinned. One or two of the class looked rather shame-faced. Hastily, Miss Clements said, "Oh, I am sorry, Finley. That was very rude of us."

She turned back to the rest of them. "And now we'll get on with the lesson."

Pie in a fight

Juliet had chosen Cookery as one of her after-school hobbies. She hadn't particularly wanted to do it, but since her dad could fiddle his Tuesday work schedule around and pick her up from school, it fitted in quite well. (The other two hobbies on that afternoon were Tae Kwon Do and Model Making, and Juliet definitely hadn't fancied either of those.)

This week they were making pastry for a blackcurrant

pie. Mrs Hilliard had brought in the filling for everyone because, as she told them, all her fruit bushes had gone berserk the year before, and she was getting rid of as many berries as she could to make room in the freezer in case the bushes went just as crazy this year.

So blackcurrant pie it was. When the pingers went off, each of the six of them took a tea towel or an oven glove to get their own pie out of one of the two ovens they were using. By the time Juliet reached the table, only one tea towel was left. She was too shy to ask Simon Parsons, beside her, to lend her the much thicker one he had thrown carelessly over his shoulder, like a real waiter or chef. So the heat of the baking tin scorched her fingers though the thin stuff of the towel, and though she didn't actually drop the pie as she slid it out of the oven, it did bang hard once on the oven bars, and by the time she had hurried it over to the table, she could see that the crust was broken right across.

Simon leaned over and grinned. "Your pie looks as if it has been in a bit of a fight."

The way he said it was perfectly friendly. Still, Juliet still couldn't think of anything to say back to him. By then, Tory and Jeremy had wandered over to see how everyone who used the other oven had done. "It'll taste just as good," comforted Tory. "My mum says things that look awful very often taste the best."

"It doesn't look *awful*," Jeremy said judiciously. "Just as if it took a bit of a knock. And if it matters to her, Juliet can swap her pie for mine before we go home. I don't in the slightest care what my pie looks like. I'm only here because my mother made me choose this club. She says that, if a man won't learn to cook, he can't expect his wife and family to stay around for long."

Simon pretended to be shocked. "Jeremy! You're never married already! And with kids!"

The teasing went on until Mrs Hilliard came over with the boxes she was giving them to take their hot pies home. "And don't forget to turn them out of the tins as soon as you get in. The kitchen will want those back, sparkling clean, first thing in the morning."

Juliet carried her pie box carefully out of the school gates, glad to see her dad's car waiting just a little way along the street.

"Good fun?" he asked, as she slid onto the seat beside him.

"Yes," she said dutifully. Then, realising that, in a way, it had been, she said again more firmly, "Yes, it was."

Words of wisdom

Mr Goodhew was talking to them about jobs. He wasn't sure how he'd ended up on this topic. It was, admittedly, something the school did tackle, but not in this, their first year. One moment he'd been taking the register, and the next he'd somehow found himself advising Prisha not to become a pharmacist simply because her parents kept telling her it was a very good job for a girl. "You would be wise to think about what *sort* of job would suit you best, before you decide on any profession at all," he told her. "You won't be choosing your examination subjects for quite a while. You've plenty of time to find out if you prefer arts, or languages, or sciences, or a mix. And only after you've settled on that should you start thinking about actual jobs."

"Is this careers advice?" asked Cherry. "My sister says

we're not supposed to get careers advice till we're in her year."

Mr Goodhew found himself nettled by Cherry's attitude. "It's never too early to get a bit of careers advice," he told her. "And since I might fall under a bus before you get the chance to hear my own particular words of wisdom, I'll offer them to you now. Here's my careers advice. Work out what you like doing most in all the world, and then look round for someone who'll pay you to do it."

Cherry was smiling at him forbearingly, as if she thought that Mr Goodhew was a thousand miles away from being able to give good advice to anyone her age.

"I'm serious," Mr Goodhew persisted. "Knowing yourself is *important*. I mean, if you like being out in the fresh air, then think of getting an outside job, maybe in farming or in forestry. If you like fiddling with things, consider being some sort of engineer, or a dentist's mechanic, or something. If, when you're bored, you always end up writing, or reading, or painting, that should tell you something about which career path you should choose."

He noticed more of them were listening than before.

"There's something else," he said. "You have to work out if you like working with other people, or if you don't. If you're a control freak, then it's best not to end up in the sort of job where you're always having to work with others in a cooperative fashion." He saw them staring at him, and thought it wise to end up with a joke. "And if you can't stand not having someone to talk to all the time, I don't advise you to become a monk in a silent order."

"Or a nun," Cherry corrected him sternly.

"Yes," Mr Goodhew said apologetically. "Cherry is right. Or a nun."

After a moment's silence, Maria felt brave enough to ask him, "So what did you work out about yourself that fetched you up as a teacher?"

He grinned at her. "I found out I was extremely bossy by nature. So teaching is the perfect job for me."

Maria turned to point. "I think that Finley ought to be a lighthouse keeper."

"Yes," Finley said. "I think I would be very good at that."

The first buzzer sounded. "Right, then," said Mr

Goodhew. "I want everyone packed for the day and out of this classroom by the time the second buzzer goes."

And because he was so bossy by nature, almost everyone was.

Forlorn

A couple of weeks after half term, Mrs Lapinska took two of her classes to the Art Gallery. They shuffled through the revolving door set in the pillared entrance, and wandered across the marble floors into the first of the galleries. Paintings of all sorts were crowded round the walls. Bewhiskered men glared down. Small children leaned against the knees of mothers in silken dresses. Families passed oddly shaped loaves along rough wooden tables. Men shouldered cannons through the deepest mud. Cracked urns spilled with unruly flowers. Red-coated soldiers wielded muskets as the bullets flew. Everywhere the class looked, there was another picture capturing a single moment in any one of a thousand different lives.

Some of the class went round the room clockwise, some the other way. One or two hurried round the gallery so fast they lapped the others.

Finley, Mrs Lapinska noticed, stayed staring at the very first painting. He wasn't there alone for long. Juliet wandered back to join him, and after the two of them had gazed at the painting for a little longer without saying anything, Mrs Lapinska was curious enough to move closer.

The painting showed a young woman gazing wistfully out of a window. Behind her, a man was sifting through a heap of accounts.

Suddenly Finley spoke. "She looks so sad."

Mrs Lapinska knew how shy Juliet was in class. She barely opened her mouth. But now she heard Juliet saying confidently to Finley, "I bet she never wanted to marry him in the first place. I bet that's why she's turned away, so he can't see her face. She doesn't want to upset him." The two of them studied the figures in the painting a little longer. Then Juliet concluded, "No, she's not at all happy. I expect she really wanted to marry someone else."

Mrs Lapinska realised she wasn't the only one who had begun to eavesdrop. Akeem and Stuart had skidded to a halt as they were going past a second time. Akeem pointed to the painting. "Maybe they're running out of money," he suggested. "He looks as if he can't get his accounts to work out right. Maybe the two of them are worried about that."

Stuart said, "No, I think that Juliet's right. I think she's wishing that she hadn't married him. He doesn't look that worried – just as if he's trying to get the figures sorted."

Alicia, who had also stopped to join the group, agreed. "They can't be all that broke." She pointed. "Look at that carpet. And all those china figures on the mantelpiece. And that's just *one* of their rooms. If he does the accounts in there, it probably isn't even one of their best rooms. If they sold even a little of that fancy stuff in the cabinet behind him, they'd more than likely be all right."

Simon and Ben had come up behind them all now, so Mrs Lapinska stepped back to leave more room. "Maybe her parents gave her all those china figures as a wedding present," Ben suggested, "and she would be embarrassed if they had to sell them."

Juliet spoke up again. "Maybe she had them in her

bedroom all the time that she was growing up."

Akeem dismissed this idea. "No one lets children have stuff that valuable in their bedroom."

"They might have, back in those days," argued Ben. He turned to Mrs Lapinska. "What do you think?"

"I think that Juliet might be right about why the woman looks so forlorn," said Mrs Lapinska. "I think that she was probably told to make a good match."

"Good match?"

"A fine marriage," Mrs Lapinska explained. "With a man who has money. And I don't think that he looks worried enough to be going bankrupt."

Most of the rest of the two classes had joined them now, curious as to why such a large group had formed in front of this one painting. Katherine said, "Maria and I have gone round the whole room. Why are you all just standing here staring at this picture? Is there something funny about it?"

"No," said Alicia. "We were just wondering about it."

"What they were feeling," Ben explained.

"And why the painter thought it was important," Stuart added. "Because it would have taken whoever did it ages to paint." He looked to Mrs Lapinska for confirmation. "I'm right, aren't I, Mrs Lapinska? This painting would have taken *hours*."

"Days," confirmed Mrs Lapinska. "Possibly weeks. Even months."

A waste?

On the bus ride back to the school, Mrs Lapinska listened to them chattering to one another about their morning.

"I loved that lady with the man's head bleeding on a tray."

"Bit harsh."

"My favourite was that puppy trying to hide under the swing in the garden. He was so *sweet*."

"I liked the miser with his piles and piles of golden coins."

Stuart called over to Finley. "You must have liked the one of that sad woman staring out of the window best. You stared at that for *ages*."

"It was the only one that Finley saw," Akeem scoffed.

"It was the first he looked at, and he stayed in front of it the whole time we were there."

"Bit of a waste!"

Mrs Lapinska found herself saying quietly to herself, "A waste? Oh, I don't know about that." She'd never had a group turn out so thoughtful on a trip to the Art Gallery. There they'd all stood, discussing *Woman at a Window* for so long. Had there been something about the painting itself that had intrigued them? Or had they been swept up in Finley's absorption? Had the boy's gift for stillness somehow proved catching?

Had Finley somehow managed, more than she ever had, to show a class how to *look* at a painting?

"What do you do up there?"

Juliet saw Finley hoist himself up to his usual perch, halfway along the wall. She kept her eye on him for quite a while. He didn't seem to do a thing. He simply sat there. In the end, Juliet's curiosity outweighed her shyness and she came close enough to ask him, "What do you *do* up there?"

Finley stared down. "Sorry?"

"What I mean is," explained Juliet, "do you sit up there so that you can *think*?"

"Not really, no," said Finley.

"Then are you meditating? Like a yogi, or a monk, or something?"

"No."

"Are you *watching* people?"

"Not especially," said Finley. Then, seeing she expected more, he added, "Though I suppose that, if a fight started, or someone fainted or something, I would notice that."

"Are you *planning* things?"

"No."

"Well, are you *worrying* about things?" Juliet asked. She thought about her own terrible worrying. It still happened all the time. Some horrible idea would drop into her head, out of the blue, and she would waste hours, sometimes days and weeks, letting it nag away at her. She knew that almost all her worries were silly and she should learn to deal with them. And yet she didn't have the faintest idea how to begin to try.

But here was Finley, shrugging off the idea that he might be sitting on the wall worrying. "No, I don't tend to do that."

Juliet couldn't help getting irritable. "So what *are* you doing?"

"I'm not doing *anything*," Finley defended himself. "I am just sitting here. I do have thoughts. But I don't actually *think* them. They just drift across my mind. I don't remember them." Seeing her look of disbelief, he added, "You ought to try it. Then you'd understand."

"All right," said Juliet. "I'll try it."

A party? Oh, that would be horrible.

Juliet hoisted herself up on the wall, a few feet along from Finley. It was quite high – a bit too high for comfort. But at least the top of the wall was flat. Juliet didn't cross her legs like Finley because she wasn't confident that she could balance properly. She simply let her feet dangle. Then she tried not really thinking, or planning, or watching, or worrying, or anything else, just like Finley.

It didn't go too well. Almost at once she found herself trying to eavesdrop on Cherry and Akeem, who were having some sort of argument. Then she found herself thinking about how Dr Yates had looked so distracted as she rushed across the grounds towards the car park earlier that day. Had something terrible happened? And that set Juliet worrying, this time about her birthday. It wasn't far off now – right at the start of next month – and Amanda, her father's girlfriend, was keeping all the plans for the day a secret. "Wait and see," she kept telling Juliet.

But always before, right since her mother's first illness, Juliet and her dad had done exactly the same thing on Juliet's birthday. They'd gone to *Bella Italia* and ordered one of the giant four-cheese pizzas to share between the two of them. Sometimes they couldn't even eat the whole thing, and had to ask for the last couple of slices to be boxed so they could take them home. Only if they did that would they still have enough room to share one of the restaurant's enormous ice cream sundaes. It was the best birthday treat because it was always the same, and Juliet knew she could look forward to it with perfect confidence. There was no chance of being disappointed because she knew exactly how, from start to finish, it was going to be.

But now Juliet was worrying that Amanda might want to do something totally different. She would be there for Juliet's birthday for the very first time, and might have fancier plans. She might even want to bring her own two daughters, Clare and Cassie, along with her. She might want them to go to a Chinese restaurant instead, or to the cinema. As Juliet sat there, next to Finley on the wall, an even worse thought struck. Perhaps Amanda would try to organise a birthday party! Juliet had overheard her saying something to her dad a while ago about the fact that Juliet didn't ever seem to bring any friends home with her.

Oh, that would be *horrible*. A party. At her own house. She'd die of embarrassment. It was all right when she was younger, way back in primary school. Juliet had one or two parties then. But it was different now that all of them were older. She didn't have those sorts of friends. She got on well enough with everyone in the class, and at the gym club, and at Junior Brass Band. Nobody *hated* her. But just to think of any of them trailing to her front door with presents in their hands, and her having to say hello, and thank them – well, she wouldn't be able to find the words. She'd just stand in the doorway like an idiot, red in the face and wishing that she could vanish into thin air. She couldn't bear it! No, she couldn't bear it.

Juliet's stomach clenched. A birthday party. What an awful new worry! Compared to that, not getting to go to *Bella Italia* alone with her dad wouldn't matter at all. She wouldn't even mind if Amanda came, and brought Clare and Cassie along with her so that, instead of choosing one of the little tables for two in a corner, like she and her dad had always done, they'd all have to sit in one of the much larger booths along the side.

But not a party! To get out of that, she wouldn't even mind if they didn't go anywhere to eat at all, and maybe saw a film instead. She wouldn't mind *anything* so long as Amanda hadn't organised a secret party. Oh, please let that not turn out to be what she was being told to 'wait and see'.

What on earth could she do?

Just come out with it

No point in asking Finley. He was just sitting, cross-legged, doing nothing on the wall. Or rather, not doing anything. Not thinking. Not planning. Not worrying. Not watching or meditating. Not doing *anything*.

Well, she, Juliet, was going to *have* to do something. She had no choice. She simply couldn't worry like this for nearly three whole weeks. She knew – just knew – that she was going to have to go home after school this very day and work up the courage to say something to her dad and Amanda. She'd pick her words carefully and try her hardest not to upset them. But she was going to say it. "I think it's lovely that you're thinking about my birthday next month. But I just wanted to tell you that, of all the things in the world that I most *don't* want, it's a proper birthday party. I don't mind doing anything else – anything at all! But you must *promise* me that you won't try and organise a party. I would hate that."

Why not? Why shouldn't she? Just say it! Just come out with it. That would sort everything out, and stop all those sorts of nagging worries that kept her up half the night. Amanda was kind. And she was trying hard. Amanda was really, really trying to be friendly, and fit in, not just with Juliet's dad, but with Juliet as well. So Juliet knew that, even if Amanda had been thinking that giving her a party would be a nice idea, she'd stop right there and then. She wouldn't carry on, not after Juliet had been brave enough to say all that. And Amanda certainly couldn't have begun to organise it already because she hadn't started asking Juliet a load of casual questions, like who did she like best at school, or in the gym club and Brass Band. Amanda might have *thought* about starting a list of people who could be invited. But, up till now, she wouldn't have invited anyone at all.

So Juliet would be safe. This stupid, stupid worry had sprung out of nowhere, just like all the others. But this one was now gone – poof! just like that! – because Juliet had settled on a plan. She'd worked it all out for herself, just sitting on the wall.

Sliding off, Juliet turned to Finley. "Well, that was really good," she told him. "I don't think that it worked exactly the same way for me as you say it does for you.

But it did work."

"What did?" asked Finley, baffled.

"Sitting on the wall," said Juliet, "just like you said." She took a couple of steps away, and then turned back to add, "I mean, I did a bit of worrying, which you don't do. And then I did a bit of planning, which you say you don't do either. But it all worked out perfectly. So thanks for that."

"You're welcome," Finley said, still somewhat confused. And he just carried on sitting quietly on the wall, all by himself, doing exactly nothing.

Like birds along a wire

"So is there something *wrong* with him?" Miss Clements asked the rest of the staff. "Or was he just born this way?"

"I don't even know which one he is," admitted Mrs Batterjee. "I haven't got a Tandy in any of my classes."

"He's the one always sitting on the wall," said Mr Goodhew.

"*None* of them should be sitting on that wall," said

Mrs Harris. "It's just a bit too high for safety. One day, someone is going to fall off and get hurt."

"It'll be Finley, then," said Miss Clements. "He's the only one I've ever seen sitting up there."

"He's not always the only one these days," Mr Goodhew corrected her. "He has a little group of silent followers now. Juliet. Ben Forster. Even that noisy atom Akeem seems to stop spinning and settle down next to them sometimes."

"Really?" Dr Yates was most amused. "So is this Finley busy creating his own little Friendship Bench along that wall?"

"Not really, no," said Mr Goodhew. "I mean, they sit there in a row, like birds along a wire. But I have noticed that they hardly ever speak to one another." His next few words astonished even him. "In fact, they're very *restful*."

Iron Bars

Cherry was pushing a very thin, tall boy from one of the years above over towards the wall. "You have to sort him out," she ordered Finley. "Tell him what to do."

Finley leaned down so he could whisper, "Cherry, I don't even *know* him, He's not even in our year. How can *I* tell him what to do?"

"You just can," Cherry said firmly. "Juliet told me you could."

She ran off. Instantly, the boy she had pushed over started to slope away, but Finley stuck out a foot to stop him. "Why has she made you come over here?"

The boy said irritably, "She's just a bossyboots. She knows my sister. And she was pulling at me. I couldn't get in a fight with her, could I? People were watching."

Finley looked round the recreation ground. "I can't see anyone watching."

"They'll have gone off to be nasty to somebody else," the boy said bitterly, and pulled his thin jacket more tightly round him against the cold, November wind.

"What sort of nasty?" Finley asked.

"They call me Iron Bars," the boy said.

"That's not so bad," said Finley. "They call me all sorts of things." He ticked them off on his fingers. "Weird. Away with the fairies. Goofy. Bubblehead. Loopy.

Cuckoo – "

"Well, maybe you don't mind," the boy interrupted Finley's litany. "But I *hate* it."

Finley changed tack. "It is an odd thing to call you," he admitted. "I mean, I know you're very *thin*, but – "

"That's not the reason," snapped the boy. "They call me Iron Bars because my name is Ian Barr."

"Well, then," said Finley soothingly, "you could say that the nickname sort of *fits*."

The boy called Ian Barr was speaking even more hotly now. It was almost a snarl. "And my dad is in *prison*. And they *know* that. That's why they think it's funny to call me Iron Bars."

"Oh," Finley said. He thought about his own dad, away in Shetland with his new wife. He hardly ever saw him anymore, the journey cost so much. Out of pure curiosity, he asked this Ian Barr, "So do you get to see him, your dad?"

"Only every second weekend," Ian muttered. "And only for an hour and a half."

"I've not seen my dad since February," Finley said. "Last time I saw him, he'd grown this beard. I didn't even realise it was him until he called to me as I was going past, looking for him at the station."

Ian Barr looked at Finley with some sympathy. He thought he would far rather get called Iron Bars than cuckoo, or weird. And he would hate to go for getting on for a full year without even seeing his dad.

"Well," he told Finley, "I'll get back now."

"Bye," Finley said.

Halfway across the recreation ground, Ian Barr looked back at the boy Cherry had dragged him over to talk to, sitting on the wall. He didn't look unhappy. Not at all. And, if the nickname Iron Bars had seemed to him to fit, even without his knowing anything about Ian's dad being in prison, then maybe it wasn't such an upsetting thing to be called at all.

Maybe, as that strange boy that some of them thought was loopy said, the nickname did 'sort of fit'.

Another day. Another mystery.

On the day of the end of term concert, Akeem came in looking dreadful.

"Akeem," said Mr Goodhew, "I'm not even sure you should have come in this morning. You look as pale as a maggot."

Cherry looked up from where she was hastily finishing up homework. "Don't worry about Akeem," she said. "He's always like this when he has to play his flute in front of people. He gets himself all horribly worked up. He hates performing. Absolutely *hates* it."

Jamie pitched in. "Yes, back in primary he used to throw up."

Mr Goodhew looked anxiously around the classroom. "Do we have a bucket? I can't see one. Terence, you're nearest to the door. Can you whip along to Mr Harley's cleaning cupboard and bring one back with you?"

He turned back to Akeem. "Sit down," he ordered him. "Take a few deep breaths. You mustn't worry so much. It's only the end of term concert."

"Don't let Mr Chapman hear you say 'only'," Cherry warned. "He won't be pleased at all."

"Well, I won't be pleased if Akeem stays in this state all day long," said Mr Goodhew.

"Oh, that's all right," said Cherry. "Akeem will be

fine, so long as Finley remembers to bring in his flute."

Mr Goodhew was baffled. "Why would Akeem's flute be at Finley's house? Do the two of them have to share it?"

"No." Cherry pointed. "There's Akeem's flute, on his desk. Finley just brings his own."

Mr Goodhew was still confused. "But Finley told me that it was the saxophone that he was playing in the concert."

"It is," said Cherry.

The buzzer rang, and Mr Goodhew realised that he hadn't even started on the register. Pushing aside the curious idea that Akeem's performance terror would be somehow assuaged by Finley bringing in a flute he didn't plan to play as well as a saxophone he did, he started to call out their names and listen for their responses.

Another day, he thought. Another mystery. Young people are so *odd*.

Ask Cherry

The mystery nagged at Mr Goodhew, though. So he took the chance during the mid-morning break to slip

along to the music practice pods, hoping to find Mr
Chapman. He was delayed along the corridors, first
by the need to confiscate at least three different pupils'
phones, then having to break up a scuffle. On one of the
seats outside the practice pods, he noticed Tory's sister
industriously inking a rather fine flowery tattoo onto her
forearm, but reckoned he had already used up enough of
the break monitoring unruly pupils' behaviour. Instead,
he walked straight past her into the first of the two
rehearsal rooms.

The music teacher was inside, and clearly busy with
the senior orchestra. Barely surprising, thought Mr
Goodhew, given that the concert was only hours away.
He knew he ought not interrupt. Still, curiosity got the
better of him. "A quick word, Henry?"

"Must it be now, Julian?" Mr Chapman responded
somewhat testily over his shoulder. But he broke off
conducting and swivelled round to face his colleague.
"As you could probably hear as you came down the
corridor, some of this lot do need a deal more practice
before tonight's performance."

Behind Mr Chapman's turned back, Mr Goodhew

could see quite a few affronted looks, some pairs of rolling eyes, and, in one case, a quite deliberately stuck out tongue.

Again, he chose to ignore the disciplinary opportunities, and only said to Mr Chapman apologetically, "Well, that's the reason, really. Akeem is one of mine, and I have to tell you that he's in a shocking state."

"Already? Oh, for heaven's sake!" Mr Chapman shook his head. "The boy gets worse and worse." A look of horror crossed his face. "But Finley's in today, surely? Oh, please don't tell me Finley forgot to bring his flute!"

Mr Goodhew took Mr Chapman's arm and drew him aside. "Calm down," he said quietly. "Just take a moment to explain to me about this business of Finley and his flute. As I understood it, the boy was down to play the saxophone, both for his own piece and in the Grand Christmas Medley."

"That's right," said Mr Chapman. "It's just that Finley also has to have his flute at the ready when Akeem gets to his solo."

"But if it's a *solo*....?"

The Head of Music was looking at him, Mr Goodhew thought, rather as if he reckoned his fellow teacher must deliberately be acting dense. But after a moment enlightenment clearly struck. "Of course!" said Mr Chapman. "This is Akeem's first concert here at Windfields, so you don't know how we work things. Didn't the set from Janson Road explain?"

"Explain what?"

"How we do it. You see, on Tuesdays I go down to Janson Road Primary to teach some of the children who are learning wind instruments. And Wednesday is Dawson Street. I've covered both those schools for years."

"I knew that," Mr Goodhew said. "But – "

Mr Chapman interrupted. "So don't you see? I taught flute to both those boys. And that's where we hammered out the only system that works when Akeem gets in one of his states."

"What system is that?" asked Mr Goodhew.

But just then the buzzer rang, and Mr Chapman broke away. "No time to explain now, Julian. Ask one of the Janson Road crew. Ask Cherry. Cherry's one of yours, isn't she?"

"Yes," Mr Goodhew admitted. "Cherry is one of mine."

But Mr Chapman had already raised his baton and begun to count his senior orchestra back into the first theme of the usual Grand Christmas Medley.

Another quick word

With the tune of *Frosty the Snowman* ringing unpleasantly through his brain, Mr Goodhew tracked Cherry down to a corner of the recreation ground. She was standing alone, with her back firmly turned towards the school building.

"I certainly hope that's not a phone you're busy with in school time," he warned as he came closer. "I have already confiscated four today."

He watched as Cherry hastily shoved something into her pocket before turning to face him.

"A quick word?" he said.

"Okay," said Cherry most unwillingly, thinking he was about to scold her.

"Mr Chapman said you could explain to me about Akeem."

"Oh, that!" said Cherry. She was obviously relieved. "What do you want to know?"

"I want to know why he's agreed to be in the concert at all, if it gets him in such a state. And I don't understand for a moment what Finley has to do with it."

"Well," Cherry said. "Basically, it's all about his mum."

"Finley's?"

"No," Cherry corrected him. "Akeem's."

"Mrs Asghar?"

"Yes," Cherry said. "You see, Akeem's mum and dad really, really care about Akeem and his music."

"Well, so they might," said Mr Goodhew. "From what Mr Chapman tells me, he is very good indeed. And I have heard him in the practice pods."

"Yes," Cherry said. "Probably that solo of his that comes up halfway through the Grand Christmas Medley." She sighed. "But poor Akeem can go to pieces when he's on a stage."

"And before, too," said Mr Goodhew drily.

"And before, too," echoed Cherry. And then, to Mr Goodhew's almost total confusion, she added, "So it really is a very good thing that Akeem's dad works nights so usually can't come, and his mother's short-sighted."

"Short-sighted? Akeem's mother? What can that possibly have to do with any of it?"

"Well," Cherry told him patiently, "that means that she can't really see what's happening up on the stage."

"But she can *hear*."

"Yes," Cherry explained. "But when poor Akeem cracks up, Finley takes over for him."

"Takes over playing his *solo*?"

"Yes. And Mrs Asghar doesn't realise. That's why Mr Chapman always makes sure Akeem gets his solos slap in the middle of the Grand Medley. That way, he can seat Finley right behind Akeem in the full orchestra, and Finley can sort of tell when Akeem is about to freeze – "

"Freeze?"

"Well, you know, *panic*, so that his mouth dries up and he can't play the notes. Finley takes over from him. Not for long. Usually for just a couple of bars, till Akeem gets a grip and comes back in again."

76

"But that means Finley has to learn all of Akeem's solos as well as his own!"

Cherry shrugged. "Yes. But he's used to it. He's always had to do that ever since Mr Chapman invented the system. He had to do it back in Janson Road, and I suppose he'll have to carry on."

"But what about when Akeem takes music exams, and things?"

"No problem," Cherry told him cheerfully. "It's only great big *audiences* he can't stand."

Mr Goodhew was astonished. "And everyone from Janson Road knows this? Except for Akeem's mum?"

"Except for her. But after all, she hears him practising the solo over and over again at home. And he is very good. She knows that he can do it. She only doesn't know he's not so good at doing it up on a stage with everybody watching."

"Nobody's ever told her?"

Cherry said sternly, "I hope you're not planning to tell her now. That wouldn't be very kind. His mum's so proud of him. And Akeem does have enough of a grip to keep pretending that he's playing even when his mouth

77

dries up too much. He always gets going again after a moment or two."

"So this weird system does work?"

"Oh, yes," said Cherry. "It works." Now, she, too, was looking at Mr Goodhew as if he were a little slow on the uptake. "If it didn't, I don't suppose that Mr Chapman would have invented it."

Three more full days!

The concert was about to start as Mr Goodhew hurried, late, into the hall. The only empty seat that he could see was in the second row, right beside Miss Willis, the Head Teacher. So he took that. He sensed her flinch as Mr Chapman cheerfully introduced the evening as 'The End of Term Concert'.

"I *do* wish he wouldn't do that," she whispered to Mr Goodhew. "It is *not* the end of term, and I dislike him giving everyone the idea that they can slacken off. There are three more full days!"

Behind him, Mr Goodhew heard Jia Li and Tansy giggling.

Mr Goodhew didn't tend to think of himself as frightfully musical. (He also didn't think that some of the performers on the stage were all that musical either.) All the way through the concert, he let his mind drift off, over the things that he still had to do, the workbooks he should get marked, the invoices he needed to hand in to the school secretary before they all packed up for the holidays. He watched the different combinations of children come up onto the stage, play their short pieces, then go off again to storms of applause. He saw how calmly Finley took his place on stage for his brief saxophone solo, and made his bow at the end. He heard the chaotic clatter as, towards the end, all of the members of the school orchestra and wind band combined came on with even more chairs and rattling music stands. He winced as Mr Chapman tirelessly checked the tuning of each group of instruments, ready for the last two pieces that would be followed by the Grand Christmas Medley.

He thought about his sister Sarah's family, because he knew that, in a few days, he would be with them for Christmas. Easy enough to buy a few luxury foodstuffs for Sarah and Dan. More worryingly, he'd not yet started on the task of finding presents for their children. He thought that Caleb, who was ten now, might like one of those hand-held fart machines he'd seen on the Bad Uncle gift site. The elder two, he knew, were always happy with money. But what about the little one, Tash? She would be five now. What would a five-year-old want? And would she burst into his room to show him her toys and games again first thing every morning? She did wake horribly early. He honestly couldn't understand how Dan and Sarah managed with so little sleep.

His musings were broken by a noisier, and far, far longer, storm of applause than any that had come before. He'd missed the Grand Christmas Medley! He simply hadn't been paying any attention at all. The only thing he'd really wanted to hear – Akeem's solo – had passed him by entirely. Mr Goodhew was astonished.

"Well," said Miss Willis, satisfied. "Another concert over. *Didn't* it go well!"

"Very well indeed," said Mr Goodhew. Then he saw Mrs Asghar standing back further along their row, respectfully waiting to let Miss Willis out first. He had no choice but to go past her. "Wonderful!" he said, and put on his warmest smile. "Wonderful! Your Akeem has such talent, Mrs Asghar."

(That was unarguable, he thought, whatever might have happened on the stage.)

"Yes," she said proudly. "I thought Akeem played beautifully tonight. We are so proud of him!"

"With every reason," Mr Goodhew said.

And, breathing more easily, he beamed at her again and left the hall.

Cunning...

Over the last three days of term, Mr Goodhew found himself tempted several times to take Finley aside and ask him quietly, "So how, exactly, did Akeem's solo go?"

He couldn't bring himself to do it. And, obviously, he couldn't ask Akeem. The only other two he felt he might be able to speak to about the matter were Cherry, and he felt uneasy about that, and Mr Chapman himself, if he could only find him.

In the end, he asked after the music teacher in the

staffroom. "Where's Henry?"

As usual, only Mrs Harris knew the answer. "He's at Janson Road Primary today. Tonight's their end of term concert."

"Will he be in tomorrow?"

"No, that'll be Dawson Street's turn."

"But he'll be in on Friday?"

"I would imagine so."

And so he might have been. But Friday was the very last day, and everything was in such chaos that the whole idea of finding Henry Chapman flew out of Mr Goodhew's mind. Then, as he was stacking all the piles of stuff that he was taking home into the back of his car, Finley himself walked past.

Mr Goodhew couldn't resist it. "In the Grand Christmas Medley in the concert," he said to Finley, "how did it go? Did you yourself end up having to play?"

He was disquieted to see the long, cool look that Finley offered him. Then Finley said, "We saxophones *all* play in the Grand Medley. We're quite important in the *Sleigh Ride* bit, and in *Santa's Coming to Town*, and even in *Five Little Elves*. And, of course, *Jingle Bells*."

Cunning, thought Mr Goodhew, and abandoned the idea of pressing Finley on the matter of whether he'd had to play his own flute to cover for Akeem. "Excellent!" he said enthusiastically, jamming the last of his boxes into the back of his car.

"There will be other terms," he told himself as he drove home. "And there'll be other concerts."

Spring Term

Just breathing

On the day before term started, Finley lay on his back on the carpet in the front room of his home. He was thinking about the full moon. It wasn't there to be studied, because it was ten in the morning. But Finley could still see the moon in his mind's eye, hanging so round and shining in the blue velvet of night.

He heard a scuffle and felt hot breath on his face. Finley opened his eyes. Turfy was looming over him, his four paws firmly placed so Finley could no longer get up from the floor unless he pushed the huge dog off. Finley knew just how heavy Turfy was, and how stubborn he could be, so didn't even try to roll away. And after a moment or two of simple staring and panting, Turfy collapsed with a bored sigh. He lay, half on and half off Finley, closing his eyes and starting on a gentle snore.

With every breath that Turfy took, Finley could feel the thick and hairy body rise and fall against his side. For no reason he could think of, he tried to match the rhythm of his own breathing to Turfy's. At first he found his own breaths came much slower than the dog's, and so he speeded up. But then he realised that, as Turfy fell into a deeper sleep, the dog's breaths, too, came slower. So Finley curbed his own until he reckoned he was breathing pretty much as slowly as he'd been before. From time to time, Turfy sighed irritably and scrabbled his paws, breaking the rhythm, so Finley had to work out how to speed up, or slow down, to get in sync with him again.

The two of them lay there for nearly half an hour before Luke opened the door. "Mum wants to know what you're doing. Are you asleep?"

Finley didn't open his eyes, but he did answer. "No," he said. "I'm just breathing."

"Sensible," Luke said sarcastically. "If you stop breathing, things can go very, very wrong."

He shut the door behind him and went back to report. "He says he's breathing."

"Well, there you go," their mother said. "I always told you Finley has some very sound ideas."

A rush for the door

Ms Fuentes looked out of the staffroom window.

"First day of term," she said, "Classes not even started, and that boy of Julian's is back on the wall."

"I must talk to Miss Willis about that wall again," muttered Mrs Harris. "It's an accident waiting to happen."

"You'd think the boy would have more sense," said Mr Brownlow. "It's perishing cold out there. That surface must be *icy*. Someone should warn him he'll get piles."

Ms Fuentes looked baffled. "Piles? Explain, please. What is piles?"

Nobody near to her offered to explain the affliction. Indeed, there suddenly appeared to be rather a rush for the door, and Ms Fuentes found herself alone. She googled *Piles*, and found an image or two. Then, gently shuddering, she, too, left the staffroom.

Horrors of which you know nothing

Mr Goodhew strolled over to Finley, who was sitting on the wall. He had a soft flat waterproof cushion in his hand. "Here," he said. "Ms Fuentes wants you to use this. She took it from the gym equipment cupboard because she's worried about you spending so much time on this cold wall."

"That's really nice of her," said Finley. "But I don't need a cushion, honestly."

"Just *use* it," Mr Goodhew said. He added darkly, "It may save you from horrors of which, in the first bloom of youth as you are, as yet you know absolutely nothing."

So Finley took the cushion and Mr Goodhew walked away.

The deep, wide and eternal waters round him

As he was running past the wall on which Finley was perched, Jeremy skidded to halt. "We're setting up a scratch game, but the other side's complaining they're one player down. Want to pitch in?"

"No. Happy here, thanks," Finley said.

Jeremy screwed his face up. "Doing *what*?"

"Nothing," said Finley.

"Are you waiting for the buzzer to go?"

"No."

"Well, what are you waiting for, then?"

"I'm not waiting for anything," Finley told him patiently. "I am just sitting here."

"You must be waiting for *something*."

"No," Finley said. "You've got me wrong. I'm not waiting for anything. I don't actually like waiting for things much, and I never have."

Jeremy was interested now. Temporarily giving up on trying to find one last person for the other team, he hoisted himself up on the wall beside Finley. "What do you mean?"

Finley shrugged. "I reckon waiting just chews up your life. You wait for term to start, and then you wait for it to finish. You wait for Christmas for far, far longer than Christmas ever lasts. You wait for your birthday for ages and it's over in one day. You wait for – "

Hastily, Jeremy interrupted him. "Yes, yes. I get it, Finley. You hate waiting."

But, for once, Finley was determined to explain himself a little more. "I like to think about the moment that is happening inside me and outside of me just at that moment. I like to pretend that I am slowing all those moments down, to pay attention to them."

Jeremy gave this a couple of moments thought before he said, "But aren't they all the same, these moments? I mean, if you're not doing anything with them, aren't they just *boring*?"

"No," Finley said.

Jeremy said decisively, "I know *I'd* find them boring. All those moments, one after another, and all the same. If I wasn't *doing* anything with them. I would be bored out of my skull. I couldn't bear it."

"Well, I can," Finley said. "I don't think that I'm bored. And, even if I *were* bored, I don't think I would mind that nearly as much as you say that you would."

"Clearly not," Jeremy said. Seeing his mates frantically waving at him from across the recreation area, he slid off the wall. "I'm off now. Sorry."

A step or two away, he turned. "Hey, Finley," he called back. "Will you be thinking about what I think after I've gone? Or will you just go back to thinking your own way about all your empty moments?"

"I'm not sure," Finley said. "I'll let you know."

Jeremy nearly said, "Well, I'll take your advice, and not be waiting," but he stopped himself at the last moment. No one was rude to Finley. And even if they had been, Finley would barely have noticed. He was, thought Jeremy, a bit like the look-out in the crow's nest of some old-fashioned sailing ship who must, from time to time, see things on the surface of his swaying world: a spouting whale, a wheeling albatross, a school of porpoises.

But mostly only the deep, wide and eternal waters round him.

High time she learned some proper manners

Julian Goodhew was sitting on a bench some way along the indoor shopping mall. It was a Saturday, and he'd been taking the horrible woolly his mother had given him for Christmas back to the shop. Now, he was sorting through his supermarket loyalty cards in search of the one he hadn't been able to find when he rewarded himself for his thrift by buying a box of chocolate peppermint creams. (The box had been on sale, and cheap enough already, but Mr Goodhew thought there was no point in having loyalty cards if you couldn't find

92

the things when you needed them.)

The sound of a raised voice caused him to look up. A short way in front of him, a man with a sturdy looking baby in a stroller was arguing with someone on his phone. "What do you *mean*, it won't be ready till Tuesday? You promised me you'd have it up and running by the end of today!"

A small child, clearly another of the man's charges, was drifting away from her place beside the stroller. In case the father was too distracted to notice if she wandered too far, Mr Goodhew kept watching.

Just then, he saw Finley Tandy walking down the mall, and as the boy made to walk round the little girl, she put out both her hands to stop him in his tracks. "See!" she said fiercely, pointing down to one of her glossy black shoes. It had become unbuttoned, and the strap was flapping loose.

Without a word, Finley dropped to one knee in front of her, and twisted the button through the tiny hole.

The little girl began to run back to the pushchair.

"Hey!" Finley called after her.

She stopped.

"Say thank you," Finley ordered.

The little girl scowled and put out her tongue at him. Her father, though he was watching now, was still too busy arguing with the garage to break off his call.

"I mean it," Finley said firmly. "Put your tongue back in your mouth at once, and I want a proper thank you."

The girl surrendered. "Thank you," she sing-songed – though a shade sarcastically, thought Mr Goodhew. He watched as, satisfied, the boy ambled on, further along the mall. He clearly hadn't noticed his teacher sitting a short way off on the bench, and Mr Goodhew didn't call attention to himself.

The short exchange came back to him more than once during the next few days. And curiosity got the better of him. On Wednesday morning, spotting Finley ambling along the corridor towards the classroom, Mr Goodhew stopped him to ask, "On Saturday, when you were in the mall, did you actually *know* that little girl who wanted you to fix her shoe for her?"

Finley expressed no surprise that Mr Goodhew knew about the short encounter. He simply answered, "No. She just sort of made me do it."

"And then you made her say thank you."

Finley shrugged.

Mr Goodhew persisted. "You didn't know her, then? Or any of the family? Not at all?"

"I'd never seen her before," said Finley. "But I did think it was high time she learned some proper manners."

"Quite right," said Mr Goodhew, pushing open the door to the classroom for both of them. "High time."

But he did wonder, as he took his seat behind his desk, ready to start the day, why Finley had never even asked him how his class teacher had known in the first place about the scene with the discourteous little girl.

Writing lies

"I just wish I knew what he was *thinking*," Mr Goodhew said, staring at Finley out of the staffroom window. "What goes on in his mind while he is sitting there, in his own peaceable kingdom? Does he feel totally at ease with the world? Or is he thinking really deep and clever things?"

"Well, if he is, they're certainly not about maths," Dr Yates replied tartly. "He does come up to scratch, but only just."

"And if he's brooding about anything in geography," said Mrs Harris, "from what I've seen of his class work he would be pretty much wasting his time."

From her usual perch beside the photocopier, Ms Leroy spoke up. "Julian," she said to Mr Goodhew. "if you really want to know what's going through the boy's mind while he's up there on the wall, get him to write about it."

"Write about it?"

"Yes," said Ms Leroy. "I find that you can learn a huge amount about their inner lives from the writing they hand in. I mean, way back in primary school young children only seem to make up all the usual weird stuff about space ships and grisly murders and sunken wrecks and brilliant burglaries. But by the time they're this age, if you ask them to write something personal, things can be very different. A lot of them are almost like adults in that they find it really hard to write lies about things that matter to them."

"Is that true?" asked Ms Clements. "*Do* adults find it hard to write lies about things that matter to them?"

"They do," said Ms Leroy. "That's why therapists ask their clients to set down what's happened, or how they're feeling, and bring it to the next session."

Ms Clements turned to Mr Goodhew. "Well, there you go, Julian," she said. "Ask him to write about whatever it is he's thinking about, when he is up there on the wall."

"Oh, yes?" said Mr Goodhew. "As his science homework? You don't think that the boy would find that just the tiniest bit suspicious?"

On the Wall

But an opportunity soon came. Less than a week later, Ms Leroy stopped Mr Goodhew in the corridor and begged him, "Julian, you're not teaching first thing after lunch, are you?"

"No," Mr Goodhew said smugly. "That's one of my free periods."

"Do me a jumbo-sized favour," said Ms Leroy.

"Take my lot for me in case I'm not back from picking something up from the chemist."

"Oh, really, Sarah! Can't it wait?"

Ms Leroy turned on him the look of a wounded fawn. "Oh, come on, Julian. The sooner I get started on these pills, the better, and they've sent the prescription through to my local pharmacy. You know that I live miles away."

Mr Goodhew collapsed. "Oh, all right. Which class is it anyway? And what do you want me to do with them?"

"It's your lot," she told him. "And you can do whatever you like. Anything to keep them quiet. Maybe look at a poem or two?"

"I can't teach poems!" said Mr Goodhew, horrified.

But Sarah Leroy was already rushing off. Just before disappearing round the corner, she called back over her shoulder, "Then get them to *write* something. Anything at all. Anything to keep them busy till I'm back."

As it happened, he had most of them anyway for the last lesson before lunch. It was their science class. As they were packing up their stuff, ready to leave the lab, he thought to warn them. "By the way, Ms Leroy won't be taking you for English first thing this afternoon. I will. So don't go to her room after lunch. We'll have the lesson here."

Akeem was startled. "You're going to teach us English?"

"After a fashion," Mr Goodhew admitted. "I'll probably just be asking you to write something."

Cherry pitched in. "What? *What* will you be asking us to write?"

Cornered, he tried to put her off. "Well, I'm not sure. I haven't settled on that yet."

But Cherry was in her usual determined mood. "Can't you think about it *now*? Give us some warning."

"Then we could think about it over lunch," agreed Ben Forster.

"And do a better job," wheedled Alicia.

That's when the idea struck. "I thought," said Mr Goodhew, "that I might just give you a title and let you write whatever you want under that heading."

"What heading?" demanded Cherry.

Mr Goodhew took very great care not to be looking anywhere near Finley when he came out with it. "I thought perhaps I might choose *'On The Wall'*."

Oh, I feel terrible. Terrible.

"Why are you staring out of the window all the time?"
Dr Yates asked Mr Goodhew. "You know that Sarah
won't get back in time. You'll have to cover for her, as
you promised."

"I wasn't looking out for Sarah," Mr Goodhew
admitted gloomily. "I was watching Finley Tandy."

"Why?"

"Because he isn't acting normal," Mr Goodhew said.
"He isn't on the wall."

Dr Yates joined Mr Goodhew at the window.
Together they watched as Finley walked in fast, half-
demented and untidy circles around the edges of the
recreation ground.

"He's been doing that ever since he came out from
lunch," said Mr Goodhew. "I think he's worrying, And
it's all my fault. I warned them I was going to ask them
to write an essay for me."

"Well, the boy can *write*, can't he?" Dr Yates said

tartly. "He can hold a pen."

"Yes, he can write," admitted Mr Goodhew. "Of a fashion. But I think that he's going crazy, worrying how much he wants to reveal about what's going through his head."

Dr Yates was baffled. "Why on earth should he be worrying about that?"

"Because of the title I've chosen. *On The Wall*. That's what I told them they'll be writing about in the lesson I'm covering." He turned his anguished face towards Dr Yates. "I am *entirely* to blame. It's just I've been so curious about what the boy does – what he *thinks* about – while he's forever sitting on that wall. And then a few days ago Sarah mentioned that people find it hard to write untruths. She said, once they get started, out it all pours – what they are really thinking, what they're feeling and what they're worrying about. So I thought I was being really cunning when I gave them the title, *On the Wall*."

"So change it," Dr Yates said.

"I can't change it now!" wailed Mr Goodhew. "It's far too late. Some of them will have been thinking about

101

what they want to write all through the lunch break."
He let out a giant sigh. "And clearly Finley has as well.
But not in a good way. Look at him! Clearly fretting
himself sick." Mr Goodhew spread his hands. "Oh, I feel
terrible. *Terrible*."

"I shouldn't worry, Julian," Dr Yates told him
cheerfully. "If Sarah's right, and the moment the boy
picks up his pen everything churning round in that
weird noddle of his spills out onto the page, he might
feel a good deal better for it. You might be doing him a
favour. It could be cathartic."

"*Cathartic?*"

"Cleansing," Dr Yates explained. "A bit of a relief.
Like exorcism, but nowhere near as scary."

"Yes," Mr Goodhew responded testily. "I did know
what cathartic *means*."

Innermost fears? Thwarted dreams?

Mr Goodhew watched Finley all through the lesson.
Still feeling that he had no choice, he'd written the title
on the board, and ordered them to get started. Most

of them claimed to quite enjoy free writing, anyway. No doubt it made a pleasant change, he thought, from scrabbling through their grubby, broken-backed copies of whichever set text Ms Leroy had chosen, searching for bits to copy out that might back up their mangled memories of what she'd told them in a previous lesson about this character's pride, or that character's cunning.

Finley, Mr Goodhew saw, kept his head down and wrote, not frantically but steadily, for the whole time. Mr Goodhew himself was a good deal less successful at spending the time to effect. He tried to put aside his fretting and press on with the coming week's lessons plans. But what on earth could the boy be setting down so busily on all those sheets of paper? His innermost fears? His thwarted dreams? A heap of relentless anxieties? Or maybe something quite different. Was he perhaps describing a series of strange religious visions? Telling about small, soothing voices deep inside his head? Once or twice, Mr Goodhew half rose, desperate to wander round the room as usual, and take a peek over one or two shoulders before settling silently behind Finley and his lengthening screed to see what was going on. But then he forced himself to stay on his chair.

Better to wait. He'd get to read it soon enough.

At last the buzzer rang, and he could gather in their work. He chivvied all of them out of the room, then rooted through the messy pile to find the only pages he was interested in. He wasn't going to bother to read any of the others. That was Ms Leroy's job.

He only planned on reading one.

Nothing of any interest whatsoever!

Mr Goodhew sat at the large staffroom table and flattened out the pages he had snaffled. The heading was the only bit that had been written neatly: *On the Wall, by Finley Edward Tandy.*

He started to read.

"Are you not having any lunch?" asked Mrs Harris. "If you don't want to go along to the lunch hall, I can offer you a spare pot of noodles."

"No, thanks," said Mr Goodhew. He read through Finley's essay from start to finish with astonishment, then turned back to the start.

"Listen to this," he told the assembled company. "One of my class just wrote it.

'I have two pictures on the wall in my bedroom. One is of Justin Masters, who is the lead singer of the Raving Fops, and I don't really like his music much but I do like the poster because it has some shiny bits at the top and when you move around the room they flash in a funny way. The other picture on my wall is a real painting of a boring man with a pipe. I don't know why it's on my wall, except that Mum says there is nowhere else to put it and she can't throw it out in case Aunt Elsie gets upset. I thought the boring man with the pipe might be Aunt Elsie's husband, but my brother Luke says that she never married. On the wall next to that are all my full attendance certificates from back when I was in Janson Road primary school and a hook Mum hammered in so that I could hang up my –'."

"Excuse me, Julian," interrupted Mr Porter. "But is there a reason why we are listening to this pedestrian drivel? Is the boy working up to something exciting on one of his other walls? A long-lost masterpiece by Titian? A stolen section of the Bayeux tapestry? A fully authenticated signed pair of his favourite footballer's underpants, framed in gold?"

"No," Mr Goodhew admitted, beaming. "It just goes on and on like this from start to finish. Nothing of any interest whatsoever!"

"And so your point in boring all the rest of us rigid with this *is* – ?" Mr Porter broke off and delicately waited for Mr Goodhew to explain.

"Well, don't you *see*?" said Mr Goodhew. "There I was, worrying myself stupid that I'd been trying to stick my grubby fingers into the poor boy's soul – "

"Not grubby, exactly." Mr Porter rebuked him gently. "A tiny bit stained, yes, from some of the things you use to clean laboratory equipment. But if you will refuse to wear the protective gloves provided – "

"Anyway," Mr Goodhew interrupted, still beaming widely. "I am off the hook."

"And hopefully we are, too," Mr Porter muttered.

"I've learned my lesson," Mr Goodhew said. "I'm never going to try anything like this again. From now on I shall leave the boy in perfect peace."

"Where he belongs," suggested Mrs Lapinska.

"Yes!" said Mr Goodhew fervently. "Where he so obviously belongs."

The honour and the glory

Mr Goodhew came into the room brandishing a piece of paper. "Good news!" he said. "Especially for Katherine and Jia Li. And for the honour of this class."

"What's that?" demanded Cherry.

"Do you remember, back in your last term in primary school, that some of you went in for something called the County Mathematics Challenge?"

Most of them looked entirely blank.

"No."

"Never heard of it."

"What is that, anyway?"

"It is a competition," Mr Goodhew explained. "You take the challenge back in top primary-"

"You mean a test? A *maths* exam?" interrupted Simon.

"Well, sort of," Mr Goodhew admitted.

"I didn't take it," Cherry announced with evident satisfaction.

"I did," said Terence. "But only to get out of the Fun Run."

Maria stared at him. "You really must *hate* fun."

"I do," admitted Terence. "I think I hate 'fun' almost more than anything in the world. It always ends up *not* fun."

"Well, you're safe now, Terence," Mr Goodhew assured him. "No Fun Runs in this school." He waved the sheet of paper at them again, and tried to drag them back to the business in hand. "But the results of the County Mathematics Challenge have just come in. And Jia Li, I have to tell you, reached Silver Standard." He grinned at her. "Stand up, Jia Li. Take a bow. Round of applause, please, everyone."

Everyone clapped frenetically, and kept on clapping till Mr Goodhew was forced to roar at them to just pack it in now, thank you, that's *enough*. He took up the thread of his good news. "And there is more! Our Katherine here – " He waved a hand at her. "Katherine reached Gold Standard!"

Because a lot of them already had palms that were smarting badly, this time the clapping didn't last so long.

It was only a minute or so before Mr Goodhew was able to add the rider, "So Katherine now goes on to the next round."

"What's the next round?" asked Cherry suspiciously. "Is it another exam?"

Mr Goodhew examined the few lines printed at the bottom of the sheet of paper he had been holding. "Well, yes. I'm afraid it is."

Katherine, he noticed, looked contented enough. But one or two of the rest of them were shuddering gently. There was a long, long silence.

Suddenly Finley spoke up. "It doesn't seem quite right," he said, "to take a very hard maths exam, and then, as the reward for coming top in it, to have to sit down and take another."

"There is the honour and the glory too," Mr Goodhew tried to explain.

But he could tell, from looking at the expressions on the faces of the class, that all the rest of them, apart from Katherine and Jia Li, were taking Finley's line on this, not his.

Bless us, Oh Master

Next day, when Finley was sitting cross-legged on the wall, Maria came up in front of him. She was just asking if he knew when they were meant to hand in their science homework, but to Ben, on the other side of the playground, the little scene looked rather as if she were standing looking up at a holy statue.

He gathered his mates around him. "Come on. Let's have a laugh."

There was a bit of whispering, then gradually, in groups of twos and threes, they drifted over towards Finley. One by one, they dropped on their knees and prostrated themselves in front of him.

Suddenly Stuart remembered a line he'd learned for a play back in primary school. "Bless us, oh master," he called out to Finley, who was just sitting smiling in amusement.

"Yes," others cried. "Bless us, oh master!"

"Bless us, please."

Alicia was passing by, and she remembered something from church about somebody's holy countenance. So she, too, dropped to her knees. "Show us your holy countenance," she pretended to beg him, even though Finley's smiling face was already there for everyone to see.

"Yes!" some of them echoed. "Show us your holy countenance!"

Mr Brownlow just happened to be looking out of the staffroom window. "Weird times," he said. "Look. Almost half of Julian's home class are on their knees on the tarmac."

Mrs Harris abandoned her pot noodles and came over to look. "So what's all that about?"

"They appear to be worshipping that Finley."

"Is that the one who nests on the wall?" asked Mr Rutter.

"Yes, that's the one."

Mrs Harris went back to her noodles. "I can't help but wonder about some of them," she said. "I truly do. Where do these strange ideas spring from?"

"If I know anything about that lot," Mr Brownlow said, "the idea will have come from Ben Fuller."

"Is that the one I'm always ticking off for racing

down the corridors?" asked Mr Porter.

"No, that's more than likely Akeem," said Mr Brownlow. "He's like a piece of popcorn on a griddle."

"And Finley is the one who exudes peace and calm and quiet?"

"Yes, that's the one."

"We ought to clone him," Mr Porter said. "Bring me a few of his nail clippings and I'll start working on it in the lab."

I got worshipped

Finley went home that day to find his mother painting the back door that he was walking towards. "You can't come in this way!" she told him. "Go round the front. I've left that door unlocked."

Finley walked back around the house and made his way through to the kitchen. He found his brother sitting comfortably at the table, eating chocolate biscuits.

"You're back early," Finley told him.

"The lecturer never turned up," said Luke. "We

waited twenty minutes, then gave up."

Their mother called in through the open doorway, "And how was your own day, poppet?"

"It was quite interesting," said Finley. "I got worshipped."

Startled, his mother stopped painting for a moment, "*Worshipped?*"

"Yes," Finley said cheerfully. "I was just sitting on the wall, and suddenly a few of them bowed down in front of me. And then the others saw, and thought it was a laugh, and they joined in. And in the end almost all of them were on their knees, pretending to worship me."

"Well, I very much doubt if that will start happening in this house," Luke warned him.

"Especially not if you go anywhere near my paint before it's dry," said his mother.

"No," Finley said calmly. "It's not the sort of thing that happens often, I should think."

His brother laughed. "To anyone except you," he said, "it's not the sort of thing that happens at all."

Serene

"I blame myself," Julian Goodhew confessed to everyone in the staffroom. "It is entirely my fault that they caught on to this idea of treating Finley as if he's some sort of deity. There he was, staring calmly ahead of him while all the rest of them were fussing away about some tiny alteration of their routine that I had just announced, and I made the mistake of asking him if he had taken the change on board."

"But, Julian," said Miss Ellerman, "how could that possibly have set all this off?"

Mr Goodhew shrugged. "It was the way I said it, I suppose. I stood in front of him and sort of slid my hands sideways up two imaginary drooping Grand Vizier's sleeves and bowed to him and asked, 'Oh, Most Serene One, did that room change announcement register with you, or must I go through it all again?'"

Mrs Lapinska chuckled. "And that was all you said?"

"Yes, that was all I said. But it was clearly quite enough to set Ben Fuller off."

"It was all right when it was just your lot outside

at break," grumbled Ms Clements. "I found it quite amusing to watch them gathering round his perch on the wall and pretending to worship him. But now it's half the school. They break stride every time they see him coming towards them down the corridor, and bow and scrape as if he'd just stepped off a cloud or something. And all the rest of them are stopping to watch, and causing logjams, and getting to classes late."

"To be fair to the boy," said Mr Porter, "he isn't trying to encourage them. He doesn't play up to it, or lose his temper. He barely even responds. He just keeps going, rather as if the whole pack of them were as good as invisible."

"Well, that's how he is," said Mrs Harris. "Imperturbable."

"Serene," said Mr Goodhew. "Which is all I said. It's just that, now, I really wish I hadn't."

But that's the truth

Juliet had never gone to anybody in school for advice on anything before. Each time the idea even occurred to her, she worried that whoever she asked would think her problem was stupid. But Finley was on the wall, as usual, and everyone who had been pretending to worship him had drifted off to watch the quarrel brewing between Cherry and Simon Parsons about how puppies should be trained. It had been getting fierce.

Juliet didn't dare climb up beside Finley in case people thought that she was trying to edge in on the joke of his being The Most Serene One. She just stood in front of him, took a deep breath, and said, "Finley, if you had two sort of step-sisters and they'd invited you to a scary film, and you knew you would hate it but they'd never asked you to anything before and you really didn't want to say no in case they thought you were being stand-offish or didn't really like them or their mum – " Losing her way in her long tangle of a sentence, she simply finished lamely, "Finley, what shall I do?"

"Say you can't go," said Finley.

"But I'll have to give them a *reason*," said Juliet. "If I don't have a good reason, they're going to hate me."

"They're not going to hate you," said Finley. "And anyway, you have a good reason."

116

"Do I?"

"Of course you do," said Finley. "You said it yourself. You told me that it was a scary film. Nobody has to go to films that scare them."

"You don't think that sounds babyish?"

"No," Finley said. "I think it sounds pretty grown up, to know what you can handle and what you can't. My mum can't watch half the stuff that's on the news. Something quite horrible comes on and the telly's off in a flash. Mum always has to keep the zapper beside her on the sofa. My dad used to say that she's so quick on the draw that she could have been a star in any of those old cowboy films."

"Well, what shall I say to them?"

"Just say you'd love to go to a film with them, but not a scary one because you'd spend the whole time hiding under your seat, and they might think you're a baby."

"But that's the *truth*," said Juliet.

"Yes," Finley said. "So it's an easy answer to remember."

"I suppose it is," said Juliet.

She was a little baffled, but she couldn't find a flaw in

his suggestion. And after a bit of reflection, she realised that she felt, if not exactly good about the idea, perfectly comfortable.

"Right," she said. "I think you're right. I'll tell them that. I don't think they'll be horrid."

"Well, if they are, then you'll know that they're halfway to being *wicked* stepsisters," said Finley. "So you'll know better than to want to spend any time with them at all."

The hobbies timetable

Katherine was looking so fretful that Juliet stopped in her tracks. She'd never dared to speak to Katherine before. Katherine was so clever. She put her hand up all the time in class, usually first. She never worried about tests, and it was obvious from the look on her face when she put down her pen at the end that she'd found them quite easy. She never forgot her gym stuff or her science overall. She never seemed to get told off by anyone for anything.

She was, thought Juliet, about as clever and as perfect

as it was possible to be. So it was odd to see her standing outside the dining hall, looking so very unhappy.

Juliet tried to force herself to walk past, but couldn't. She had to say something to Katherine and, after a huge effort, out it came. "Are you all right?" she asked. "You look a bit upset."

"I am upset," said Katherine. "I'm really upset. I've just been told I can't do chess club after the half term hobbies switch-about."

"That's a bit mean," said Juliet. "Is it because they don't have enough chess boards? It's easy enough to draw a pretend one on paper. My grandpa says they did that when he was in the navy and they wanted to play chess or chequers but the board wasn't about."

"It's not that," said Katherine. "I know they have more than enough chess boards."

"That *is* mean, then," said Juliet. She thought for a moment. "I had a problem too," she told Katherine. "And I told Finley about it. It was a problem about my family, and he sorted it out for me. I did what he suggested and it worked perfectly. Everyone was happy. I think that now, if I had any problems, I'd go and talk to Finley."

"Right, then," said Katherine, "I will."

Katherine saw no reason to hang about. She went straight up to Finley, who was sitting on the wall. "Juliet sent me," she told him. "She said that you would sort out my problem for me."

"Really?" said Finley. He was a little startled. "Is it a problem about hating scary films?"

"No," Katherine said, baffled. "Why should I have a problem about scary films?"

"No reason," Finley said. (Like Juliet, he was a little wary of Katherine.)

Katherine made an effort not to roll her eyes at Finley. "The problem *is,*" she said, "with the half term hobbies switch-about. I want to choose new things. I want to pack in country dancing and folk singing, and do ceramics and felt-making instead, and now they're telling me I can't do chess club as well."

"But I thought people are allowed to choose three."

"They are. But Mrs Batterjee is telling me I can't."

"That seems a bit mean of her," said Finley. "Did she give any reason?"

"Oh, yes!" Katherine said scornfully. "She told me

that chess club and felt-making are both on Tuesdays, straight after school, so either I would have to choose between them or she would have to spend hours trying to rejig the hobbies timetable."

"That seems quite reasonable," said Finley.

"Of course it does," said Katherine, misunderstanding what he meant entirely. "After all, how long can it take someone with half a brain to rejig a timetable?"

Finley tried to be tactful. "Not everyone is as quick as you at doing things like that," he offered.

"Mrs Batterjee is a *teacher*," said Katherine.

"Yes," Finley agreed. "But Mrs Batterjee teaches different stuff. She might not be any good at rejigging."

Seeing that Katherine was staring at him in a somewhat hostile manner, he tried a different tack. "Maybe you have to learn to choose in life," he told her. "Decide which, out of felt-making and chess club, you want to do most, and choose that. Then do the other one next time."

"Next time!" Katherine said scornfully. She turned away and then, remembering her manners, turned back, not very enthusiastically, to thank him. After that, she stomped off, and Finley thought he might have overheard her muttering something to herself about hoping he'd been more useful about scary films. But then the buzzer rang, and with relief he slid off the wall and hurried over to the queue at the south door, where he thought he would be more safe.

Doing exactly nothing

Jeremy came down the steps from the dining hall and wondered which way to go. He'd sat at the same table as Jia Li and Maria over lunch, but he didn't want to follow them. His usual friends, Jamie and Stuart, were both off school for the day. Jamie was at his grandfather's funeral in Wales, and Stuart wasn't well.

Jeremy was so used to spending break and lunch time with Jamie and Stuart that it felt weird to have both of them gone at the same time. He didn't feel that he could easily walk up to any of the other groups milling about.

What to do? Where to go?

On the far side of the recreation ground Finley was sitting on the wall, swinging his legs, and doing nothing.

He never joined a group of friends at break or after lunch, but nobody talked of Finley as if he were some sort of Johnny-No-Mates. No one thought twice about it. From time to time, someone might wander across and speak to him for a moment. Then they would drift away, back to the friend or group that they'd been with before.

Finley never looked lonely, or out of things. He was just Finley sitting on the wall.

Jeremy wondered if he should walk across and sit beside him. Or maybe a little further along the wall. If Finley could look as if he were perfectly happy, and not at all left out, then surely Jeremy could too. In the end, Jeremy plonked himself down on the bench under the staffroom window. Now he was facing Finley. If Finley could sit on a wall and look perfectly normal and relaxed, then so could Jeremy on a bench. And he was far enough away for no one to notice that he was copying what Finley did.

But Finley didn't do anything. He simply sat there. Jeremy kept his eye on him for a while, but there was nothing to copy. Nothing at all. So Jeremy's attention moved to the football match in front of him. It was quite clear the two scratch teams were in the middle of some huge discussion, with frequent bursts of laughter. Jeremy watched them for a while. Then a bird landed almost no distance away, close to his feet. He watched the bird scrabble for a moment or two on the tarmac, find something that he fancied, and gobble it down. The bird flew off, and Jeremy paid attention to where it went. It flew to the fir tree just beyond the school fence, and back from there onto the roof of the lunch hall. There was a missing slate on that, and Jeremy wondered if he should go along to tell Mr Harley. When Jeremy's dad had pointed out to the Bahmanis next door that there was an almost permanent spill of rainwater from their front gutter, they'd sounded grateful enough.

Above the roof, clouds scudded past and Jeremy watched them, wondering why everybody was so quick to claim they looked like proper shapes. "Oh, there's a wheelbarrow!" they'd say. And, "That one looks exactly like a teacup." To Jeremy, they mostly looked like clouds. Then yet another floated over, and even Jeremy could see that it was like the illustration of Caspar the Ghost in one of his old books. He watched it for a while, till it changed shape, wondering whether or not he really believed in spirits and phantoms and things. His parents told him that the whole idea was nonsense. But ghosts were fascinating. And ghost stories were so interesting that he'd like nothing better than to be able to believe in them.

Except he really, really wouldn't ever want to see anything properly ghostly. That would freak him out. He'd never dare to sleep alone again. He'd have to ask his brother to move back into the room they'd had to share for too long anyway. That would be terrible.

The buzzer sounded. Startled, Jeremy got up from the bench. Break time had gone so fast that he could hardly believe it. On the way over to the double doors, he found himself quite near to Finley. Up until now, he'd always wondered how Finley could spend so much time sitting up there on the wall, doing exactly nothing.

Now he knew.

Spot on!

Katherine came into the classroom, singing.

"You sound very cheerful," Mr Goodhew told her.

"I am," said Katherine. "You saw me yesterday. I was extremely fed up. We're supposed to be able to choose three of the hobby clubs, and Mrs Batterjee had told me that I couldn't do ceramics, felt-making and chess club. She'd said I couldn't do them all."

"Not for any *mean* reason," Mr Goodhew reminded her. (They had already been through this.) "Only because two of the clubs happened to take place at the very same time."

"And she said that she couldn't rejig it,"

"These things aren't easy," Mr Goodhew said.

"They're not that difficult, either," said Katherine. "You only have to think it through."

She burst into song again.

Mr Goodhew stared. "So has she done it?"

"*She* hasn't," Katherine said, with just a touch of scorn. "But *I* have."

Mr Goodhew was astonished. "Seriously? You've managed to rejig the entire hobbies timetable so that everything fits in and everyone is happy, including you?"

"Spot on!" said Katherine triumphantly.

"And Mrs Batterjee has seen it? And approved it?"

126

"Yes. She said that she was dead impressed. And I can do all my three things."

"Then well done you, Katherine!" Mr Goodhew said. "I can see why you did so well in the Maths Challenge, and why Dr Yates has such high hopes of you."

"Well," Katherine admitted, a shade unwillingly. "I might have done all the rejigging, But, to be fair, it was Finley who suggested it."

"Really?" said Mr Goodhew. He'd never thought of Finley as someone with a sophisticated view of the possibilities of alterations in a school timetable. "It was Finley's idea to rejig?"

"Well, sort of," said Katherine. "It was Finley who pointed out that Mrs Batterjee was probably rubbish at rejigging."

"Really? Did he say *that*, exactly?"

Katherine did a brain search. Then she amended her claim. "He said he thought that rejigging the timetable might not be that easy."

"Not *quite* the same," said Mr Goodhew. But he knew when it was time to put an end to a discussion. "I'm glad that everything has worked out so well," he said.

Katherine dropped her voice so no one else inside the room could hear. "I do still worry a bit," she admitted. "I worry that I might upset Dr Yates by deciding I want to make things out of felt all day when I leave school, instead of doing maths."

"I wouldn't worry about that for a long while yet," said Mr Goodhew. "Plenty of time to think about that later."

He picked up the register and swung around to face the class. "Right," he said firmly. "Into your places, please, everyone, and let's get going."

Tantrum

Akeem had a tantrum. Everyone who had come up from Janson Road had seen him lose his temper before, but Mr Goodhew was astonished. He'd walked in to find Akeem standing in the middle of the room, scarlet in the face, wheeling his arms around, and growling – literally *growling*.

Mr Goodhew asked Alicia, who was nearest to him, "What on *earth* is the matter with Akeem?"

"He's gone off the deep end," said Alicia. "Our old teachers used to call them his outbursts."

"Is that right?" Mr Goodhew said. "What set him off?"

"Nobody knows," said Alicia.

But it was obvious that everyone had a theory.

"He broke his new pen," Ben explained.

"Stuart jogged his elbow by mistake," said Jamie.

"He left his science homework in his bedroom," Jeremy said, "after he'd spent hours on it."

"I heard his baby sister isn't very well," said Juliet.

"Maybe he hates his new haircut," Simon Parsons suggested. "It certainly doesn't suit him."

"It's just a temper," Katherine said scornfully. "He definitely should have grown out of them by now."

Akeem was still growling. His arms windmilled about so fiercely that one of them hit Maria as she inched past. She pushed him hard as she said, "Ouch!" Akeem didn't even notice.

Mr Goodhew tried to take control. "Akeem!" he told the boy sharply. "Stop that right now and pull yourself together."

Most of the class turned to face Mr Goodhew, and one or two of them, he thought, were looking at him rather pityingly.

"That isn't going to work," Cherry told him.

"No, that won't work at all," said Jamie.

"He doesn't even hear what you're saying," Stuart explained. "Not when he's in the middle of one of his outbursts."

Akeem's face was now so furiously red he looked as if he might explode, and he was panting hard. Mr Goodhew said worriedly, "What *do* I do, then?" He turned to Cherry. "You were at Janson Road. What did the teachers there do?"

All of the pupils who had come from Janson Road Primary pointed at Finley.

"Sorry?" said Mr Goodhew, mystified.

"They sent him off with Finley," Cherry explained.

"To the changing rooms," said Jamie. "Or, if there were people in there, they went along to the janitor's cupboard."

No one else added anything. That seemed to be the sum of it. So Mr Goodhew asked, "What happened after that?"

Maria shrugged. "Well, after a while they'd both come back to the classroom."

Mr Goodhew spread his hands. "That's it?" he asked, incredulously. "That's the advice? Just send him off with Finley, and he'll come back again later?"

"Yes," said Maria. "That is what happens next."

Mr Goodhew turned to look at Finley.

Finley sighed. "Oh, all *right*!" he said, a little grumpily. He walked up between the desks and caught hold of one of Akeem's flailing arms. "Come on!" he told him firmly. "Time to go."

Dragging Akeem behind him, Finley left the room. Mr Goodhew stared after them. He could still hear Akeem growling all the way along the corridor.

"They won't be that long," Alicia assured him. "Still, you might as well get started on the register."

Mr Goodhew knew when he was being given good advice. With some relief, he sat down at his desk and started on registration.

Oh, it was nothing

"What was that quite extraordinary noise coming from your room this morning?" asked Mrs Batterjee. "If I'd not been carrying a rather heavy printer, I would have poked my head around the door to see if everything was all right."

"Oh, it was nothing," Mr Goodhew said. (He had recovered.) "Only Akeem, having an outburst."

Mrs Harris looked at him with real concern. "I certainly hope that Finley was in school."

Mr Goodhew stared. "How did you know about that?"

"My husband used to teach at Janson Road," Mrs Harris said calmly. "They were quite used to Akeem boiling over. What set him off this morning?"

"Nobody knows," said Mr Goodhew. "There were a lot of theories, but none of them made sense. What sort of things used to set him off in his old school?"

Mrs Harris tried to recall some of the odd things about Akeem her husband had told her over the supper table. "Harry told me Akeem can't stand being shown other people's scabs," she said. "And that Alicia of yours was in his class back then and once came off her bike quite badly. She kept on shoving her rather spectacular scabs and grazes under Akeem's nose to annoy him." She thought some more. "Oh, yes, and he hates hearing the word 'weasel'. Harry said that always sets him off. Don't ask me why."

"Are they *all* totally baffling when you learn more about them?" asked Ms Fuentes. "Or only a few?"

Nobody wanted to answer that, so there was silence for a while. Then Mrs Harris wrapped up the conversation by saying comfortingly to Mr Goodhew. "Still, you were lucky Finley wasn't off today."

Seeing through someone else's skin

Mr Goodhew stopped Alicia in the corridor as she was off to the lunch hall. "Can I ask you a question, Alicia?"

She looked at him as if he might be feeling ill. After all, weren't teachers *always* asking questions? Wasn't that their job?

"What I want to know," said Mr Goodhew, "is what

it is, exactly, that Finley does to get Akeem to calm down."

Alicia relaxed. That was an easy enough question to answer. "I don't know," she said. "I just know that he does." Seeing that Mr Goodhew wasn't satisfied, she added helpfully, "But you could ask Akeem. Or Finley."

Suddenly Mr Goodhew wondered why he had asked Alicia, instead of going directly to one of the two boys concerned. He didn't feel quite right about questioning Akeem about his tantrum, and the way it ended. So in the end he went in search of Finley.

He found him in the changing rooms, struggling with a knot in one of his laces. Not wanting to ask him anything so personal in front of the few other stragglers hanging about before the second lunch sitting, Mr Goodhew asked Finley, "May I borrow you for a moment?"

Just at that moment the knot came loose. "I'll wait," said Mr Goodhew, "while you get sorted."

Finley drove his foot into the troublesome shoe, and tied the laces. Mr Goodhew led the boy outside, and further along the corridor, into Mrs Lapinska's deserted art room. "It's about Akeem."

Finley looked startled. "But Akeem's fine now," he said. "He's been all right all morning."

"Yes," Mr Goodhew said. "But I am curious. I know it isn't really right for me to ask you, but he did seem in the most terrible state when you took him out of the room, and I did want to ask you how you calmed him down."

"He always calms down in the end," said Finley.

"I realise that. But I just wanted to know what line you take with him."

"Line?"

Just for a moment Mr Goodhew wondered if the boy's apparent bafflement was some sort of act. With just a hint of irritation, he said to Finley, "What do you *do*?"

"Do?"

"Yes. When Akeem gets in this state. The others say it's you who always calms him down. The question's simple. All that I'm asking, Finley, is what do you *do*?"

He watched as Finley's face cleared. "Oh, that. Well, nothing, really."

"Nothing?"

"Not really, no. I mean, I sit with him. And in the end, he just stops growling and flapping his arms about all by himself."

"You don't *say* anything?"

"Not really, no. I mean, he isn't listening, is he? Even if I did say something, it would only make him more cross." Finley stared up at Mrs Lapinska's art room notice board as if in search of further inspiration. "When he was younger I suppose I sometimes used to pat him."

"Pat him?"

"Yes. Just a bit. Quite lightly. That used to help a little." Finley sighed. "But he's too big for that now." Suddenly on his dignity, he added hastily, "And so am I."

"Right," said Mr Goodhew. "So what you're telling me is that you don't have any particular magic system to get Akeem out of his rages. You simply sit beside him for a while."

"Yes," Finley said. "That's about all there is to it."

Not sure what to say next, Mr Goodhew moved back a pace or two. "Well, thank you for explaining all that," he said, even though nothing was any clearer to him than it had been before. "I won't keep you any longer.

136

Off you go."

He stood and watched as Finley made his way down the busy corridor, flinching whenever the imaginary ball being kicked by a small bunch of much older pupils seemed to be hurtling his way. How frustrating, thought Mr Goodhew, not to be able to see through someone else's skin. Other people were such a mystery. First Akeem. What on earth had set him off, and what on earth was he thinking – if indeed he was in any state to think at all – while he was having his outburst? And, in his own quiet way, Finley was even stranger. What was it about him that could just accept that he should be the one to calm Akeem, not in a formal way, but just by being himself and sitting close to him?

And had there been a moment when Finley had been seen as the right one for the task? And had he minded that he'd been the chosen one, and that, from that moment on, it would be seen as no one's job but his? Did the boy wonder if there was anything odd about himself, for that to have happened way back in primary school?

Shaking his head, Mr Goodhew went back to the

empty classroom. He didn't want to mingle in the staffroom over the lunch hour any more. He simply wanted to be quiet and *think*.

Still waters

What *was* it with the boy? Mr Goodhew had always thought it was as well that everyone had private places, especially a child. He could remember how painful much of childhood had been: the sensitivities that you could have about wearing the wrong clothes, or feeling sure that you were the wrong height or shape, or had the wrong sort of face. At that young age, whatever you were like, you wanted to be different. You probably wanted your parents to be different as well. And any brothers or sisters in the same school. Less obvious. Nothing to be stared at. Nothing about them that might get you teased. It was amazing, Mr Goodhew thought, how much could be going on inside a child's head without the rest of the world having a clue. Whole storms of misery and anguish, yet nothing showing on the face. Not even anguished writhing at the desk, or fiddling with pens and pencils.

Not all of them were that way, of course. With quite a few, in his experience, their upset showed up at once. You saw it round them, like grey mist, as they walked into the classroom in the morning. You could approach the matter. "Alan, could I have a little word?" And when you asked them, in the privacy of the empty corridor, "What is the matter? You look a little rattled. Has something bad happened?" out it might pour – the details of the bullying on the way to school, the much loved dog that was run over in the street, the horrible, horrible row between the parents overnight, in which the word 'divorce' kept echoing along the landing.

And yet there must be some (not many – Finley was the only one that Julian Goodhew had yet come across) who seemed so much themselves each day – so *Finley-ish* (no other way to put it) – that it was hard to think of them as having lives at home at all, let alone worries and moods. Surely, if there were any upheavals – possibly even cataclysms – going on inside the boy, *something* would show on the surface?

Hearing a knock, Mr Goodhew turned to find Mr

Porter peering round the door.

"I came to see if I could borrow a few matches, Julian. My burners are so clogged I've got through my entire store."

He took the small box Mr Goodhew offered him and made to leave. Then he turned back. "A penny for your thoughts? You did look miles away."

"Oh, nothing really," Mr Goodhew said. "Only that Finley of mine. I can't make head or tail of him. He really is 'still waters running deep'."

"Might not be," Mr Porter said. "Still waters don't by any means always run deep. Sometimes, you'll find, still waters just run *shallow*."

I'm just there, like you

Finley was wondering much the same about himself that evening. Miss Clements had had a go at him in science. "Oh, Finley, is that really the best that you can do?" Then Mrs Lapinska had picked up his art work and sighed. She hadn't said a word. But he had definitely heard her sigh.

And later Dr Yates had just come out with it. "You'll have to buck up a bit, Finley. I know you could get more of a grip on what we're doing if you tried."

Three of them, all in one day.

His mother sent him out as soon as he got home. "Turfy's been stuck in the house almost all day. He must be desperate. Don't even bother to hang up your jacket, Finley. Take the poor animal down to the park at once."

He didn't mind. It was a nice enough afternoon, and he and Turfy took the long way to the park, along the canal. Once through the gates, Finley let Turfy off the lead, and the two of them wandered around. Sometimes Finley followed Turfy along the gravel paths and in between the trees, and sometimes Turfy followed him. Turfy was nosing in clumps of grass, and lifting his leg against tree trunks while Finley was thinking about what had been said to him by Miss Clements and Dr Yates, and what Mrs Lapinska might have said if she hadn't been too gentle by nature to do so.

It was quite clear that all three teachers were dissatisfied with him.

Finley sat down. He pulled up several grass stalks

and began to plait them. The criticisms, he reckoned, weren't altogether fair. He paid attention in class. He did his homework. It wasn't his fault that he wasn't clever, like Katherine and Jia Li and Simon. He didn't have their sort of brains and that was that, just as he wasn't as sporty as Terence and Maria. Or as good at art as Anthony.

On the plus side, thought Finley, he wasn't noisy and distracting, like Akeem could be. Or bossy in the same way Cherry was. He was –

What, exactly?

Feeling a Turfy-sized bump, he turned to see that his dog, too, had given up on moving about and plumped himself down almost on top of Finley. The two of them leaned together, each feeling the warmth and comfort of the other's body as the moments passed and shadows crossed the grass.

What am I? *What?*

Finally it came to him. "I'm like you, Turfy. I'm just *there*, like you."

Felt mouse. Or gerbil. Possibly.

Katherine came up to Finley and put what looked like a small heap of soft grey material on the desk in front of him. "There you go."

Finley inspected it. "Is it a mouse?"

"Yes," Katherine said. "Or gerbil. Possibly."

"It's very good," said Finley.

"Yes," said Katherine. "It's the first thing I did in felt-making class, so I thought you should have it as a gift from me."

"A gift? But why?"

"Because you sorted out my problem for me."

"Did I?"

"Yes," said Katherine. "You were the one who told me to go home and re-jig Mrs Batterjee's hobbies calendar so I could do felt-making and ceramics and the chess club too."

"Was I?"

"Yes," Katherine said. "You were. Only four weeks ago. Just before half term. Don't you remember?"

"No," Finley admitted. "I don't remember that at all."

"Well, never mind," said Katherine. "You can still have the felt mouse." She eyed her handiwork a little critically. "Or gerbil."

"Mouse, I think," Finley told her. "Definitely mouse."

His clear cut line on what the creature was instantly banished all of Katherine's concern. "Well, there you go," she said. "A lucky mascot. For the end of term tests."

"End of term tests?" said Finley. "Are we having end of term tests?"

"Don't you pay attention to *anything*?" asked Katherine. Then she sailed off.

Teasing

Alicia was feeling bored enough to try to tease Finley. She saw him by the window, staring out at the rain, and came across to ask, "What are you doing?"

"Nothing," said Finley. "Just looking out of the window."

"But you've been standing here all through break."

Finley turned marginally – just enough to raise an

eyebrow at her. "And your *point*?"

"Well, it's not normal," said Alicia.

"I'm watching the rain," said Finley. "What is so strange about that?"

"There's nothing to watch about rain," insisted Alicia. "Either it stops, or it keeps coming down. But you've been standing here right since the buzzer rang, and look as if you could watch it for a whole *week*. Or even *month*."

After a moment, Finley said, "I think I probably could. There's something so *easy* about rain, the way it just keeps falling down and down. It would be hard to want it to be any different."

"So you're not even wishing it would stop?"

He shook his head.

"Or get even worse?" persisted Alicia.

"No," Finley said. "I have no views about it at all."

"That's what's not normal," said Alicia. (She was getting irritable with him now.) "All of the rest of us are either wanting it to carry on, so we can stay inside, or wanting it to stop, so we can get out there and do something else. You are the only person in the world

145

who can just stare out of the window without having any feelings about it at all. So what is *wrong* with you?"

"Nothing is wrong with me," said Finley. "It's just I'm not like you. I don't have to have feelings about everything that happens around me. I don't have to care about everything. I don't even have to have views on everything."

Alicia took another tack. "What if it didn't stop raining for three whole months? Would you still be standing here, staring out of the window, just like now?"

"Probably not," said Finley. "If it kept raining for three whole months, I'd probably be expected to help out."

"Help out?" asked Alicia.

"Well, yes of course," said Finley, and he grinned. "After all, by the end of three months I expect Mr Goodhew and Cherry would be getting us to build an ark."

Infuriated, Alicia turned away and went back to her desk. The teasing of Finley hadn't gone well. In fact, she rather felt as if he'd done a better job of teasing her than she had of teasing him.

Tennis ball

Finley was wandering through the park with Turfy. As usual, Turfy was rooting in all the laurel bushes behind the tennis courts, hoping to find one of the many balls that had been lobbed over the high wire fence by accident, and never found because the players hadn't thought to search through the branches. Sometimes when Turfy couldn't reach a ball he had spotted, he would sit and stare up at it stubbornly till Finley noticed his dog was no longer anywhere beside him on the walk, and came back to shake it down.

With a tennis ball clamped in his jaws, Turfy was happy. On the rare occasions when the owner of the ball saw what was happening and called for their property to be returned, Finley would have to prise the damp and slimy ball out from between Turfy's jaws. Turfy would let out a persistent throaty grumble that sounded like a rather threatening growl. Some of the players were so successfully fooled by this that they handed their now somewhat unsavoury ball back to Finley. "No, really. It's fine. Safer to let him keep it."

On this occasion, Finley had walked further than usual without noticing Turfy's absence. He was worrying about the end of term tests. They'd come about much faster than he could have imagined after Katherine first mentioned them. He'd already taken six, and the last of them were coming up over the next couple of days. He knew he hadn't done a lot of work for any of them, but it was not till he'd seen the question papers that it came home to him how very little effort he must have made.

Still three to go. Maybe if he worked hard tonight, he'd have a chance to drag his overall mark up just a little.

Then he remembered what Mr Rutter had said to them. "No point in thinking that leaving it till the last minute to get your head down is going to do you any good."

Miss Clements had said much the same. "It's slow and steady that does the job with revision. Trying to cram everything in the night before an end of term test simply won't wash."

So it was hopeless, really. He had left the business far too late. He might as well relax.

Thorns in lions' paws

Tests and exams were one thing. The only person Finley could let down was himself. But in the case of sports teams, he'd learned the hard way that others in the class could have the strongest views. Cherry had made her own opinions on the matter very clear often enough before, and she was coming out with them again now.

"Oh, buck up, Finley! Pay more attention, will you? If you'd moved faster, you could have stopped that ball, easy-peasy!"

"Excuse me, Cherry," Mrs Hilliard called over. "Who is taking this lesson? You or me?"

"You are," admitted Cherry, but she added sullenly, "Though you must agree that if Finley *cared* a bit more, our side would definitely have won that point."

"I *do* care," Finley argued. "I am doing my best."

Cherry just couldn't help it. "Well, your best is simply not good enough. You should shape up a bit."

"Cherry!" warned Mrs Hilliard. "One more word from you, and – "

"Oh, all *right*!" said Cherry. She turned her back on

Finley, still muttering under her breath.

After the lesson, Juliet found herself walking faster
to catch up with Cherry, who was striding crossly off
the field. Usually, if Juliet had something rattling round
her head that she would like to say, she bottled out at
the last moment and just stayed silent. But she felt so
grateful to Finley for –

For what?

For simply being Finley, she supposed. In any case,
she was much braver than usual. "You mustn't think
that Finley isn't trying," she told Cherry firmly, trying to
defend him. "He's just not good at sports."

To her surprise, Cherry slowed down, but not to
take what Juliet said seriously. More to dismiss it out of
hand. "It *isn't* that. I wouldn't mind if Finley were just
a butterfingers like Terence. Or couldn't run for toffees.
But there is nothing wrong with Finley at all. Nothing!
His problem is that it just doesn't *matter* to him which
side wins. He can't get *into* it. He doesn't even *try*. If ever
a ball just happens to end up anywhere near him – " She
shook a finger at poor Juliet. " – and no one who wanted
their team to win would ever pass him one deliberately

– he simply stands around like a spare pudding, waiting for someone to come along and take it. He doesn't have a single *forkful* of team spirit in him. He might as well not even be on the same playing field as the rest of us. He might as well be a *hermit,* halfway up a *mountain,* in the *wilderness,* sitting cross-legged in a *cave!*"

Juliet didn't dare argue. No, not with Cherry. But at the mention of a hermit's cave she suddenly remembered a coloured stamp that she'd been given way back in Sunday School, to stick in one of the blank squares in her little book of bible stories. It was a picture of a monk, sitting outside his cave and gently cradling a lion's foot in his own lap.

"Like St Jerome," she said. "Pulling the thorn out of the lion's paw."

"I thought it was Androcles who did that," said Cherry, momentarily distracted.

"Well, Androcles might have done it too," Juliet offered peaceably.

"See?" Cherry said. She was clearly still feeling irritable. "There are obviously lots of them who go around like Finley. And I wish the whole pack would shove off and live in caves all by themselves and not muck things up for other people."

Juliet was sure there must be far less drastic solutions to getting hopeless people off the sports teams Cherry cared about. But Cherry was striding ahead now, pushing open the doors to the changing rooms, and it seemed safer to fall back and say nothing more.

Two cardboard boxes

On the last day of term, Mrs Harris stopped Finley and Alicia as they were off to the lunch room. "Can I borrow the pair of you for two seconds?"

Neither dared to object. They followed her along the corridor to her home room. Inside, a group of the oldest children in the school were horsing about and making a good deal of noise.

Mrs Harris ignored them. Pointing to two cardboard boxes on her desk, she said to Finley and Alicia, "I wonder if you'd mind taking these to the car park for me."

Alicia gave Mrs Harris a bit of a look, and Mrs Harris

said, "I know exactly what you're thinking, Alicia. But I would like the boxes getting to my car *intact*. And I would also quite like to get home tonight." She waved a hand at the unruly bunch in front of her. "So I would like my stuff to be carried by two people who are still in a halfway to sensible mood, and won't end up chucking my keys around the car park as an end of term laugh."

Alicia picked up the smaller of the two boxes. Finley picked up the other. Mrs Harris laid the car keys on top of Alicia's box and opened the door for them.

Alicia and Finley set off along the corridor with their burdens.

"If this weren't the very last day of term," Alicia grumbled, "I would have *said* something."

"I shouldn't worry," Finley comforted her. "I think that look on your face as good as did."

Plumbers and socks and other matters

The next morning, Mr Goodhew came back into school to tie up one or two loose ends and bring home all the stuff he hadn't thought to take back with him the day before. As usual in holiday time, the school seemed strangely quiet. The corridors seemed longer and the air more settled. The pictures and notices on the wall somehow stood out more clearly.

Mr Goodhew spent less than half an hour in the building. A few of the things he wanted were in the staffroom, but most were in the physics laboratory or in his class's home room. While he was rooting round for items he was sure must still be somewhere in his cluttered cupboard, his eyes kept being drawn to the wall that ran along the west side of the recreation ground.

The wall that Finley Tandy was forever sitting on.

Even the wall, thought Mr Goodhew, seemed strangely abandoned without Finley stolidly parked on it. Mr Goodhew stuffed the last of what he wanted in his bag, and then, instead of leaving by the north door that led directly out to the car park, he found himself making for the south door which the pupils used in termtime to spill out into the recreation area.

It was locked.

Mr Goodhew surprised himself. Retracing his steps

along the corridors, he dumped his heavy bag by the north door and walked all the way around the outside of the building until he reached the wall he had been thinking looked so deserted without Finley settled on it.

Mr Goodhew hoisted himself up into Finley's place.

And there he sat. His first thought was that, though the morning was mild, the stone beneath him felt chilly, even through his sturdy trousers. He remembered that Juliet had told him Finley did nothing when he was on the wall. "He doesn't plan anything, or worry, or think, or anything. He says he simply *sits* there."

Mr Goodhew had a really good go at simply sitting there. He couldn't do it. First he noticed a missing slate on the dining hall roof, and wondered if anyone else had seen and reported it. That led him on to thinking that he still hadn't called the plumber to give his boiler its annual service, which was already late. The idea of being late set him off wondering how bad the traffic was likely to be on the following day, when he had to drive to Thetworth for his dental appointment. And while he was in Thetworth, maybe he should buy socks, because ever since he had teased his mother for always giving him socks for Christmas, she'd made a point of giving him other stuff – anything – even stuff (like last year's woolly) that no one in his right mind would want. Stuff he had always ended up returning to the shop.

But never socks.

And now he was almost out of them. He was down to three or four fast-thinning pairs, and most of those had growing spuds in the heels. From plumbers and socks, he started worrying about other matters of all sorts. Thoughts tumbled, pell-mell, through his head. Things to do. Things not to do. Things he still had to think about, including sorting out the physics schedules for the term to come. Which, now he thought about it, was only three weeks away. So even if he tried to work on the schedule for a full hour or so each day, that would still mean that by the time he –

Mr Goodhew couldn't stand any more of it. Laying his hands flat on the wall, he hastily slid off.

"The boy's *extraordinary*," he told himself. "Extraordinary. I don't know how he does it. If I'd had to sit there for another moment, my brain would have boiled over, truly it would!"

Summer Term

Oh, the bliss of it!

The first morning of term was always busy. Pretty well every member of staff was in the staffroom. "Has anyone seen the key to my locker?" "Why is this printer not working? Is it out of ink *already*?" "Has someone moved the tea bags?" "Oh, surely *somebody's* seen a pile of thirty maths books lying about the place!"

Into this chaos walked Mr Goodhew. He looked close to ecstatic. "I'm going to tell you what the problem is," he declared. He was speaking so loudly that everyone in the staffroom realised at once that this was a public pronouncement. Mrs Harris looked round from her locker, into which she'd been neatly packing her tubs of noodles. Mr Porter stopped riffling through his folders. Dr Yates put down a stash of papers to pay attention.

"The problem is," said Mr Goodhew, "that we have got things totally topsy-turvy. We treat the very things we ought to be encouraging as *punishments*."

"What things?" said Mrs Hilliard.

"Well, silence for one," said Mr Goodhew. "Wouldn't it be wonderful if we had a bit more silence around the place? If we could get them to appreciate peace and quiet. Revel in it, almost, the way that we do. Revere it. Pretty well *wallow* in it if it ever happens." He spread his hands. "But how are we ever likely to get them to treat being quiet as anything other than an unpleasant discipline when one of the things we do to show them we've had enough of their poor behaviour is snap at them to be quiet?"

"I do see what you mean," said Miss Clements, "but when the noise in a classroom reaches the levels of a drunken street riot, what are we supposed to do, except demand that they pipe down?"

"Good point," said Mr Goodhew in his turn. But he fell silent only for a moment before bouncing back. "What about privacy, though? Privacy is important. Everyone wants to be by themselves once in a while. Being alone is *good* for you. And yet what do we do? We use isolation as a punishment. We actually send them out of class to *sit by themselves*. Think of it! Once again, we treat the very thing that we would love to do ourselves, and it would be useful to encourage in them, simply as a punishment. Imagine! Being by oneself for half an hour or so! Alone and undisturbed. In this building. Oh, the bliss of it! The sheer and utter *bliss*!"

Nobody spoke for a moment.

"Julian," said Mrs Harris. "Are you feeling quite yourself this morning?"

"I'm feeling fine," said Mr Goodhew irritably.

"It's not his fault," said Mr Brownlow. "Don't blame poor Julian if he's gone odd. It's all because he's had to come back for one more full term of that weird Finley Tandy. That's what's set all this off."

And realising that this was true, Mr Goodhew's fine argument seemed, even to him, to crumble into dust.

Lesson in progress

Mrs Harris went into the store cupboard a little way down the corridor from the janitor's room. She was looking for a new ink cartridge for the printer.

Inside, she saw someone sitting hunched on a stool. Though Mrs Harris could only see the girl from the back, she recognised her. "Katherine?"

As there was no response, Mrs Harris tapped her on

162

the shoulder. Startled, Katherine spun round.

"Katherine," said Mrs Harris sternly, "are you wearing earbuds?"

Katherine nodded.

"As you well know, earbuds are strictly forbidden in this school," said Mrs Harris. "And what are you doing lurking in here in any case? What lesson are you supposed to be in now?"

"I am in a lesson," Katherine explained. "I'm doing maths."

"In here?"

"It's the best place," Katherine explained. "I'm in my very own maths group now, and this way I never get disturbed." Then, worrying that this particular argument had lost a little of its thrust by Mrs Harris's arrival, she added as politely as she could, "Well, hardly ever, anyway."

Mrs Harris looked round the tiny space, all shelves and storage tubs. "Does Dr Yates *know* about this?"

"Well, yes," said Katherine. "She's the one who suggested it in the first place."

A sudden deafening grinding noise almost drowned

out Katherine's last words.

"What on earth's that?" gasped Mrs Harris.

"Oh, that's the water pipes," said Katherine. "They'll keep on doing that till Mr Harley bashes them hard with his broom. Then they calm down. That's why I wear the earbuds."

"This isn't right," declared Mrs Harris. "This isn't right at all. You can't spend lesson time in here. It isn't healthy. For one thing, you're unsupervised, which is completely unacceptable. And for another, there is no fresh air. I'll speak to Dr Yates, but you can't work in here again."

Katherine, she saw, was looking quite distraught. "Oh, please don't send me back in there with all the rest of them!" she cried. "Please don't! It's awful! I don't get to do any of my own maths at all. I spend the whole time with them going on at me. 'Oh, Katherine, can you explain this, please?' 'Oh, Katherine, is this right?' 'Oh, Katherine, Dr Yates already tried to explain this to me twice. I *still* don't get what I'm supposed to do with this bit here.'" Katherine spread her hands. "Oh, *please* don't send me back!"

Mrs Harris stood in a quandary. In the end, she relented. "You keep the door a little open," she insisted, "and I will sort you out a sign."

"A sign?"

But Mrs Harris had gone. Five minutes later she came back along the corridor, bearing a sheet of cardboard on which she'd written the words, LESSON IN PROGRESS. DO NOT DISTURB, and used a short length of dental floss to hang it over the doorknob.

"Now be an angel, and pass me the box of ink cartridges on that third shelf down."

Katherine handed over the box of cartridges, and both of them, satisfied, went back to work.

Peaceable Kingdom

Juliet was sitting on the floor of the spare room, emptying drawers. Cassie and Clare were coming for the whole weekend for the first time, and Juliet's dad had suggested that he and Juliet might take some of the old toys and games that no one wanted any more down to the charity shop to make a bit of room for any stuff that

Cassie and Clare might want to leave for their next visit.

The first pile grew of its own accord. No one played *Go Fish* or *Ludo* any more, and half the dolls and planes and cars and little animals were broken anyhow. A lot of them would end up in the bin.

The second pile took longer. Juliet had a soft spot for *Snakes and Ladders* because she liked the faces on the snakes. Then she pulled out her favourite game of all: *Peaceable Kingdom*. You chose a token. There was a prince, a princess, a handsome woodcutter, a milkmaid, a soldier, a woman with a basket of apples and a cheerful young tramp. The squares on the board showed endless traps and problems: highwaymen, hedges of thorns, high walls, quicksands, fierce beasts, more robbers, awkward stepping stones. You had to get through each of them by throwing the exact right number with the dice. And if you reached the end, you found yourself safe at last in the Peaceable Kingdom.

She wasn't ever giving that away. She might not have played it for ages, but she was keeping it. Oh, yes. Juliet was definitely keeping that.

For *ever*.

Tell her it's homework

Mr Brownlow was sitting at the staffroom table, toiling over three enormous sheets of graph paper, each covered with smudged pencil notes and signs of rubbing out. Every few moments his frown would deepen, and he would push one of the sheets of paper to the side and pull another closer.

"Are you trying to work out next year's timetable?" asked Sarah Leroy. "Surely it would be easier to do that on a computer. There must be programmes for it."

"I've tried that and I just got more lost." Mr Brownlow sighed. "It gets worse every year. I've spent hours on it already, and I'm still hitting problems."

"Give it to my Katherine" suggested Mr Goodhew. "The child's a whizz at this sort of thing. She sorted out the hobbies timetable for Mrs Batterjee overnight."

"I can't do that," said Mr Brownlow. "How can I go up to one of the pupils in your class and just hand over the most difficult job of the entire school year?"

"Tell her it's homework," said Mr Goodhew cheerfully.

On The
Handsforth-Kuperschmidt Hypothesis

Mr Brownlow did try to resist. But the idea was too tempting. He couldn't bring himself to actually *lie* to Katherine, but he did try to make the idea sound attractive. "It isn't *homework*, exactly," he told her when he tracked her down inside her tiny cupboard. "But Mr Goodhew thought that you might like to have a go at it."

Katherine took the sheets of paper that he offered her, and her eyes gleamed. "It looks dead interesting."

"He thought you might think that," said Mr Brownlow, trying to put as much distance as possible between himself and the idea of giving someone in Year Seven such a huge job.

Katherine laid the sheets of paper aside and pointed to the book that she was studying. "I'll have a go at it as soon as I've finished this chapter."

Mr Brownlow leaned down to see the title of the tome she had in front of her. *Some Thoughts on the Handsforth-Kuperschmidt Hypothesis*.

"Oh, right," he said.

Somewhat deflated, he trudged off along the corridor.

What's normal? Who's normal?

Jeremy walked through the door to find almost the whole class in a semi-circle around Katherine, who was sitting at her desk, her fingers firmly in her ears and her eyes fixed on a book.

"What's going on?" he asked Tory.

"It's Katherine," said Tory. "She's sitting there reading that book."

"So?"

"Well," Tory said. "Look at the title."

"How can I?" Jeremy asked. "For one thing, the book is wide open, and for another, there are so many people round her that I couldn't get close enough to see what the book is called, even if I tried."

Ygor turned from his place in the front row behind Katherine. "It's called, '*Some Thoughts on the Handsforth-Kuperschmidt Hypothesis*,'" he told Jeremy.

Jeremy came out with the weird, old-fashioned thing

169

his grandfather tended to say whenever Jeremy talked about some new app on his phone. "What's that when it's home with its boots off?"

Emma turned round to join the whispered conversation. "Don't you think Katherine can be a bit scary?"

"Scary?"

"When she's doing maths like this. I mean, it's worrying to think about her brain."

"Think *what* about her brain?"

Emma was irritated. "You know exactly what I mean. Her brain can't be normal, can it? Not if she can read a book like that."

Now Jeremy was feeling combative. "What's *normal*? Who is *normal*?"

"I am," said Emma. And so are Ygor and Tory." She looked to see who else was close. "And Anthony there. And Maria, and Finley."

"Finley's not normal," argued Jeremy. "Finley's like Katherine. His brain is odd."

He'd said it a bit too loudly and Finley turned round. "You realise I'm not deaf?" he challenged Jeremy. "I *heard* that. And my brain couldn't be more different from Katherine's. Her brain must have a million wheels inside it, all oiled up and spinning round so fast they set off sparks."

Jeremy put on a *Gotcha!* face. "Not if they're oiled up, like you just said. Well-oiled wheels wouldn't make sparks."

Finley was not deterred. "All that I'm saying is that Katherine's brain and mine could not be more different. Her thoughts shoot about everywhere, and she always gets to the answer faster than anyone else, and she is always right. And my brain sort of lies there, gently floating about, not doing anything much unless I absolutely force it to make an effort."

He turned back to the group who were still watching Katherine. And that's how Mr Goodhew found them when he came in to take the register. "Back to your places, please."

Reluctantly, they moved away from Katherine. Curious, Mr Goodhew reached out to raise the front cover of the book she was reading just enough to lean down and read the title.

"*Some Thoughts on the Handsforth-Kuperschmidt Hypothesis*?" He made a face at Katherine. "Scary!"

"That's all I said!" announced Emma, glaring at Jeremy. "That is *all I said.*"

You will go far

As they were all trooping out of the room at the end of registration, Mr Goodhew called Katherine back.

"So," he said. "How did it go? Did you manage to spin all Mr Brownlow's straw into gold for him before daybreak?"

When Katherine stared at him blankly, he realised that she probably hadn't been raised on fairy tales, the same way he had been. "It's just a story," he assured her, "*Rumpelstiltskin*. But I was referring to your working out the timetable for next year."

"Oh, that," she said. "It wasn't too much of a problem. We got that done last night."

Had she stayed after school? He couldn't help but ask her, "You and Mr Brownlow?"

"No, no," she said. "Me and my dad."

"Is he a maths whizz as well? Is that where you get it from?"

She shrugged. "Don't know. He runs a trucking service. So he has to know exactly where all his lorries are, and which route they're coming back on, and what they can pick up on the way. Maybe that helps."

"Maybe it does."

"Anyhow," she said, "we got it done." She added with a smile, "And yes, before the break of day."

Mr Goodhew shook his head. "You will go far, Katherine," he told her.

But already her face was clouding over. "I'm still not sure about some bits of it, though," she said. "I mean, I still think that if we moved one of Ms Fuentes' Year Eight Spanish lessons into one of the pods, then the Year Nines could have had double maths on Tuesdays instead of two single sessions set a day apart, and that would have been much better."

"Better for people like you, perhaps," observed Mr Goodhew dryly. "But maybe not for one or two of the others."

Once she was safely out of the room he repeated what

he had said to her with even more conviction. "Oh yes, indeed, Katherine. You will go far."

Parents' Evening

As Mrs Tandy took her place on one of the empty chairs in front of him, Mr Goodhew shuffled his papers until his notes on Finley were on top. Then he looked up and beamed. "Finley. A *lovely* boy," he'd started off, "and a real asset to the class." He paused, inspecting Mrs Tandy's face for any sign of disbelief or suspicion. After all, they were already well into the third term of the year, and it wasn't as if her Finley had so far shown himself to be in any way a high-flier. (Especially in group sports. Miss Ellerman could not have made that more clear.) "What is particularly noticeable about him," Mr Goodhew continued, "is his *tranquillity*. Has he always been this self-possessed and calm?"

"Yes," Mrs Tandy told him, smiling. "Right from the start. He was the easiest baby in the world."

"And his capacity for being alone," persisted Mr Goodhew. "That is unusual, too, in someone his age."

"I used to worry about that," Mrs Tandy admitted. "But then I realised that it was for real. He didn't *want* to join in with the others all the time. In fact, he seemed to treat the times he was alone as something rather precious." Again she smiled fondly. "He's still like that, you know. Sometimes he drifts into our front room and lies on the carpet for a couple of hours, and we have no idea at all what's going through his head."

"I'm told that feeling comfortable with solitude is actually a sign of emotional maturity," said Mr Goodhew. But then he noticed that the line of parents in his queue was growing longer. "However, if we can move on a little, I might suggest that Finley's tendency to be *so* very comfortably content with everything around him is not quite so wise."

Mrs Tandy began to look worried.

"I mean his rather easy-going attitude towards his work," Mr Goodhew explained. "I'm rather concerned that Finley isn't pushing himself enough."

Mrs Tandy asked, "What does he say to you when you tell him that?"

And Mr Goodhew suddenly had to face the fact

that he had *never* said as much to Finley. He had a trace memory of Ms Yates saying something in the staffroom about the fact that the boy should be making more of an effort. And he was pretty sure that Miss Clements had mentioned she had scolded Finley more than once about his somewhat uninspired (not to say shoddy) homework. But, if Mr Goodhew was honest, the whole idea of anyone making representations of that sort to Finley himself in person seemed to him seriously odd – like telling a yogi on a rush mat that he should be running a marathon, or advising a hermit that he should come down from his mountain eyrie to start up a business company.

Even, he thought, a bit like telling a saint that he should shape up and try to do a little better.

Mercifully, at that point the sound of a chair all but splintering into pieces a short way behind her caused Mrs Tandy to turn. Seeing the queue of parents waiting for their turn with Mr Goodhew impelled her to reach for her handbag. Mr Goodhew couldn't, in all honesty, wrap up the meeting by saying that he'd have another go at speaking to Finley on the matter because, till then, he hadn't had any goes at all.

But he could fudge.

"It's not as if Finley won't understand the importance of making every effort that he can," he said. "They all know that the results of this term's coming exams make a significant difference to which classes they can take next year."

"I do hope you're right," she said. But Mr Goodhew could tell, just from her dubious tone, that Mrs Tandy knew her son better than anyone, and that the hope she spoke of was a thin and feeble thing.

Park gates

Finley was ambling home from the park that evening, on Turfy's last walk of the day. Turfy was happy enough, with the nice bright yellow tennis ball he'd found a few minutes earlier clamped firmly in his jaws. They were nearing the park gates when Finley saw the tall thin boy that some of them called Iron Bars lingering beside one of the taller bushes, clearly just wasting time.

Finley slowed down. That's when he saw the three Year Ten boys who were leaning against the entrance pillars, and guessed that Ian Barr was nervous about going past them. Would he turn back, and walk the whole way across the park to the gates on the other side, just to avoid them? Or was he summoning up the grit to give it a go and try to get past them?

It didn't look as if he were going to do either, so Finley called over to him. "Hi, Ian."

Ian looked at him blankly, and Finley realised that he didn't recognise him from the conversation they had had by the wall. He pressed on anyhow. "Coming out these gates? Going my way?"

Ian looked doubtful. Then he looked at Turfy. Finley could almost see him calculating that the odds of getting through the gates without trouble were a little better now. Another boy, and a huge dog.

"Okay," he said, embarrassed.

Just as they walked together past the end of the line of bushes, nearer the gates, Finley reached down and prised the tennis ball out of Turfy's mouth. Turfy at once launched into the resentful rumbling grumble that sounded so much like a warning growl. He kept it up as they walked past the three boys, and only when Finley and Ian were round the corner did Finley give the ball back.

Neither boy spoke until they were at the very end of the next street. Then Finley turned to Ian. "I go this way now."

Ian pointed ahead. "I'm down there."

"Bye, then."

"Bye," Ian said. It was quite obvious he wanted to say more, even though probably just, 'Thanks'. But since the word did not come out, in the end Ian just said again, "Well, bye."

Ms Fuentes' cat

Ms Fuentes came into school with red and swollen eyes. The minute she walked into the staffroom, she was surrounded.

"Oh, Mariana! What on earth's the matter?"

"What's *happened*?"

"Can we help?"

Ms Fuentes shook her head. "I'm sorry. I know I'm being silly. But last night I had to take my cat to the vet

179

and – and – " She burst into sobs again. "And I have had her for so long. Years! Since even before I came to this country."

"Oh, dear me. That is terrible. I am so sorry, Mariana."

"Small wonder you're upset."

"Do you feel up to things today? Or should you be going home till you feel better?"

"No," Ms Fuentes said. "I think that home is worse without my Bella. I would prefer to stay here."

And so she did. Somehow Mrs Harris managed to nip into each of Ms Fuentes' classes before she reached them to tell them that Ms Fuentes had lost her precious cat and they were to be no trouble through the entire lesson. "Not a peep! Not from *any* of you, not on any excuse at all! Or you'll be answering to me, and I can warn you that it won't be pretty."

So Ms Fuentes managed to get through the morning. But after lunch she crumpled on one of the chairs halfway along the corridor, tears streaming down her face.

Cherry told Jia Li, "Go and get Finley. Quick."

Jia Li didn't argue, and Finley wasn't hard to find. He

was just sitting on the wall.

"You have to come," Jia Li told him. "Ms Fuentes needs you."

Assuming it was something to do with homework, Finley slid off the wall and followed Jia Li. When he saw Ms Fuentes weeping, he sat down beside her.

"We can go now," Cherry said confidently.

Over the last few minutes before the buzzer rang for classes, lots of the pupils, and more than one of the teachers, walked down the corridor. Finley and Ms Fuentes were sitting quietly side by side, and since Ms Fuentes was no longer crying, nobody had a reason to stop and speak.

Finley was seven minutes late for his science lesson. "Where have you been?" demanded Dr Rutter.

Cherry got in first. "Finley was busy," she told Dr Rutter. "That's why he's late. He has been doing something for Ms Fuentes."

If Dr Rutter had gone on to ask Cherry what, exactly, Finley had been doing for Ms Fuentes, Cherry would have been quite unable to explain. And so would Finley. But Dr Rutter had been in the staffroom when Ms

Fuentes came in that morning, so he didn't ask.

Closer to calm

The staffroom was abuzz.

"Finley? Just sitting next to her? And patting her?"

"So Henry says. Just sitting there and patting her hand."

"And she was crying?"

"Weeping her heart out. It's that cat of hers. It seems she's had it ever since she came here from Zaragoza."

"He does that, Finley does," said Mr Goodhew. "Sits next to people and just calms them down. He's been sent along to sit next to Akeem more than once."

Mrs Batterjee asked curiously, "*Who* sends him, Julian? Is it you?"

"Not exactly," Mr Goodhew admitted. "More that bossy Cherry. But she's dead right. It works. The boy just has something about him. He's soothing. He has this gift of being there, but not there, if you see what I mean."

"No," Mr Brownlow said. "I don't see what you mean at all."

"I do," said Miss Clements. "You know how religious people say that being silent is like being closer to God. Well, being close to Finley is like being closer to calm." She chuckled. "That's probably why the ones who know him go through that regular performance of kneeling to worship him."

Mr Brownlow was frowning. "Are you trying to tell me that they think the boy is *holy*?"

"No, not at all." Since Finley was 'one of his', Mr Goodhew had felt obliged at this point to take over the explanation. "But they do recognise that he is sort of detached. He's there, but part of you can't help but feel that, for all that you can see him sitting right in front of you, he's actually *elsewhere*. And that sheer peacefulness he carries round with him tends to rub off on people. I see it all the time in class."

Mr Brownlow remained entirely unconvinced. "I expect the lad's just putting it on."

"Putting it on? You mean, acting that way for effect? No, not at all. He isn't showing off. There's not a single speck of 'Look at me!' in Finley. He would have just sat down beside Ms Fuentes and patted her hand, and he'd have thought nothing of it except that she was there, and he was there, and he knew it would work." Ignoring the disbelieving look on Mr Brownlow's face, Mr Goodhew kept on. "They *all* know it works, especially those of them who came up from Janson Road. They've been in classes with him since they were four or five. They don't think anything of it. Cherry or someone will simply have seen Mariana crying on that chair in the corridor, and sent for Finley to sort her out."

"It really is that simple," Miss Clements assured the still frowning Mr Brownlow.

"It does seem to be," agreed Mrs Harris.

"The boy would appear to be a soothing beacon of calm," Miss Clements said thoughtfully. "If only we could use some form of micropropagation to grow a few more of him. We could all do with one in our classes."

"Way back in first term Mr Porter suggested trying to clone him," Mrs Batterjee remembered. "But clearly nothing came of that."

"More's the pity," said Miss Clements.

"I shall be very sorry to lose him," Mr Goodhew said.

"Who gets him next year, anyway?" asked Dr Yates.

"Not sure yet," Mrs Harris said. "The sets aren't arranged. All I know is that I could do without that noisy number, Ben Fuller." She turned to Mr Goodhew. "And I think it's time those twins of yours were separated, Julian."

"Jamie and Cherry? I reckon both of them can handle that."

"I'm not sure I could look at Simon Parsons' hair for long without sneaking behind him with a pair of scissors," admitted Miss Ellerman.

The conversation drifted on. And by the time that Ms Fuentes came in to fetch her coat and bag, ready to go home, no one was talking about Finley any more. Or Ms Fuentes.

Or her cat.

A Stranger

On her way home that day, Juliet walked round a corner and almost bumped into someone smaller than herself, purposefully striding in the other direction. She wore the same bright turquoise top and grey skirt that Juliet had worn for years at the same primary school. At Hill Top Juniors.

The two passed one another and the girl walked on. But Juliet couldn't help stopping and turning to stare after her. That could have been me, she was thinking. That's how I must have looked to anyone who happened to walk past me in the street two or three years ago.

She thought about herself back then. That Juliet. It seemed light years ago. She felt as if she were another person now. Not just grown older and taller, and wearing a different uniform, but a completely different person. That Juliet from before seemed so very distant – far, far, far away – like someone she'd once read about in an old story book.

If she were to bump into her old self now, she wouldn't recognise her. Not at all.

Why, that old Juliet would seem a total stranger.

High time to buck up

The following morning, Mr Goodhew was still giving

thought to the conversation in the staffroom. He was supposed to be marking papers while supervising the class through a wet break, but mostly he was watching Finley, and dwelling on the words he'd used to try to describe to Mr Brownlow how soothing the boy could be: 'He has this gift of being there, but *not* being there, if you see what I mean.'

He was watching an example of that now. It was quite obvious that most of the pupils milling about in the classroom were very aware of who was in the group around them, who was listening to what they said, who would quite like to get a little nearer to somebody else – or further away.

Not Finley. The closeness, or distance, of others didn't seem to impinge on the boy's consciousness at all. It seemed to Mr Goodhew that, if Finley chose to acknowledge someone's presence, then he did; but, till that moment, they might have been nothing but a shadow that fell momentarily across his desk, or perhaps the slightest graze of air as they went past him.

How did someone of that age – indeed of any age – get to be so much at peace? And was that, wondered Mr

Goodhew, the state of mind that all of us would choose to be in if we could? If we were capable? Not to go rushing through life as if we were always trying to get on to the next bit, or the best bit. Just calmly being who we are, and where we are, at that particular moment.

For Finley Tandy seemed to carry absolute contentment with him. Mr Goodhew thought back to Finley's mother's clearly supposing that it was Mr Goodhew's job to warn Finley that he should perhaps be pushing himself a deal harder. And she'd been right to think that. Mr Goodhew realised that he had to face it. He'd let far too much time go by already. He would really have to tell Finley it was high time to buck up and make an effort to work harder.

Perhaps the boy's contentment was a little *too* catching.

Hopeless!

So Mr Goodhew bit the bullet. First, he asked round the staffroom in the vague hope that the problem might magically have solved itself. Then, since it hadn't, he tackled the boy himself. "Finley, can I have a little word with you at first break? Come along to my lab."

He half expected the boy to forget, but, sure enough, a couple of minutes after the buzzer sounded, Finley appeared in the doorway. Mr Goodhew led him over to a couple of stools at the end of a work bench. "Finley, I want to talk to you about the exams."

"Exams?"

"The end of year exams. It isn't very long now before you'll have to sit them."

Was the boy listening? His eyes were fixed on Mr Goodhew's face, but the unblinking gaze suggested that, far from hearing the announcement as a warning, Finley was merely taking a mild interest in what his home room teacher had to say.

Mr Goodhew ratcheted the lecture up a notch. "Finley, they're *looming*, these exams. And they're *important*. I have been asking around the staffroom, and although pretty well everyone who teaches you admits that you are rolling along all right, I did strongly get the feeling that everyone suspects you're coasting, and they think you could do better if you pushed yourself."

Finley was still watching him, expressionless, and Mr Goodhew felt a little uncomfortable.

"We all think that it's maybe time you pulled out the stops a bit."

"Pulled out the stops?"

"Made more of an effort," Mr Goodhew explained. "Like on an organ in a church. If you pull out the stops, more noise comes through the pipes."

"Oh, right."

Mr Goodhew waited for more. Knowing how comfortable Finley could be with silence, he waited longer than he would have done with anyone else in the class. Maybe the idea of working harder, doing his very best, would take longer to sprout inside Finley. Or was the boy thinking very differently? Maybe Finley believed that he had every right to coast along, doing just well enough to keep most of the teachers happy, not feeling that he had to exert himself further than that. Maybe, deep down inside himself, Finley knew he not only had no desire to be top of the class, or anywhere near it, but also no real need to even feel that he was doing his best.

He was so *different*. Already Finley's personality, his

character, appeared more fixed than that of any of the others in the class. Unlike him, all the rest gave the impression of still being changeable. Mr Goodhew could easily imagine any one of them deciding overnight they somehow wanted to be different: maybe kinder, or more industrious, more ambitious, more brave.

Not Finley. Finley was immutable. Doggedly, unflappably himself. All year Mr Goodhew had watched the boy soothing other people's troubled souls and casting his cloak of tranquillity over a series of trivial but bitter class arguments.

And look at him now! Merely by his unruffled silence he was letting all of the air out of the balloon of Mr Goodhew's intended ticking off.

Oh, it was hopeless. *Hopeless!*

"Off you go."

Not a barn dance

And if the end of year exams were looming, that led to a further question Mr Goodhew took to considering as he pulled out of the car park at the end of the day. Who would get Finley in their home room next year? He wouldn't fancy Dr Rutter's chances of coping with the boy. Finley's sheer inaccessibility would frustrate the man utterly. Nor was he sure that, after a week or two, Sarah Leroy would be any keener. And as for Mr Porter...

He pulled out onto the bypass. How about Miss Clements? Possibly. Or Mrs Lapinska?

Mr Goodhew was just one roundabout away from his own street before he realised that he had been running through the question solely from each possible class teacher's standpoint. It had never occurred to him that Finley might have a problem.

Why was that?

Because the answer was obvious. Finley wouldn't. Finley himself would just go sailing on without any problems at all. It was other people who got unnerved about sitting next to someone so impenetrable. How often had some in the class changed places while Finley sat tight? Mr Goodhew mentally listed the conversations he had suffered throughout the year with those in the class who, for all they seemed to like Finley – even be fond of him – had, after a while, asked to be moved away from sitting next to him.

Tansy had been the first. "He makes me feel as if he's just *being there* for me," she had complained.

"Being there for you? What do you mean? Like reminding you of homework, or telling you it's time for lunch, or something? What sort of 'being there for you'?"

"I don't know!" said Tansy. "It's just that, when we have to sit together, I feel that Finley is – "

She broke off.

"What?"

"I can't describe it," Tansy wailed. "It's just I always *feel* it."

"You barely have to sit together much," said Mr Goodhew. "After all, this is only your home room."

"It's still too much," complained Tansy. "Oh, please, Mr Goodhew! Can't I *move*?"

Jeremy had been equally unable to say why he, in turn, was asking to change places.

"What's wrong with staying beside Finley?" Mr Goodhew had asked him. "Is he annoying you?"

"No."

"Teasing you?"

"No."

"Distracting you?"

Jeremy was beginning to sound sullen now. "No. He's not doing anything at all. It's just I really don't want to sit by him any longer. I've sat by him for almost a whole term, and I want to move."

Simon Parsons had been next. "I don't know why you put me next to him in the first place," he complained. "I was perfectly happy, sitting by Alicia. We got on perfectly well."

"As far as I can see, you get on perfectly well with Finley, too," said Mr Goodhew.

"Maybe I do," said Simon. "But I want to move."

"This classroom is not a barn dance," said Mr Goodhew. "People can't just keep changing places."

"I don't see why not," said Simon. "You let Tansy move next to someone else. And Jeremy. So why am I the one who has to stay in the same place all the time?"

So Simon was allowed to move.

Then it was Emma. Then Ygor.

"Don't fret about it," Mrs Harris had suggested when

Mr Goodhew was moaning about the problem one day in the staffroom. "Some of them are just better off, sitting alone."

"But Finley doesn't have a problem, sitting next to people. In fact, short term it usually proves a boon. It's just that other people have a problem sitting next to him for a long time."

"Well, that's a problem," Mrs Harris said.

So Finley sat alone. He didn't seem to notice he was by himself now all the time, let alone mind. And then, one morning, there was Juliet, sitting in the empty desk beside Finley. Mr Goodhew didn't say a word about it. He took the register as usual and saw them off to their classes.

Next morning Juliet was there again.

And she had sat there ever since.

Levels of quietness

Did people like Finley have *levels* of quietness, wondered Mr Goodhew. At parents' evening Mrs Tandy had said that he sometimes lay on the carpet in their front room for hours on end, doing nothing at all. Did that sort of physical quietness lead to an even deeper level of mental quietness in the boy? And did he seek that? Mr Goodhew tried to remember way, way back to when he himself had been in nursery school, and all of them were forced to lie on mats after their lunch for – how long would it have been? ten minutes? twenty at most? – with no toys and no talking. He was quite sure that he'd been driven nearly crazy by this enforced daily 'rest'. No doubt forever twitching and fidgeting, itching for the time to be over.

He had *hated* it.

Breakfast with Luke

On the first morning of the school exams, Luke stayed in the house later than usual so he could cook a breakfast for Finley. "All set?" he asked his brother. "Head stuffed with enough Spanish and English to see you through the day?"

"I only want cereal," said Finley.

"Tough," said his brother. "Mum said you had to

have a proper cooked breakfast before you left for school. It's more than my life's worth not to give you this egg on fried bread and these sausages."

"Sausages?" said Finley, brightening. "How many do I get?"

"Two."

Finley peered into the pan. "Not all three of them?"

"No. That burst one at the back is mine."

In between mouthfuls, Finley confessed to his brother, "I'm not like you. You can remember things. You can look at a page and try to remember it, and most of it sticks. Things just slide round in my head. I can't get a proper grip of them when I want them. And some of them just slip out without me knowing till I go to look for them."

"You do all right," his brother said. "Your school work might not be all that good, but it's not all that bad either. You'll be all right, I promise. Just keep chugging on."

On an impulse, Luke stuck out his fork to hand over his own burst sausage. And out of gratitude for this, his brother's somewhat limited vote of confidence in his academic capabilities, Finley promptly handed it back.

Results

The end of term exam results were handed out ten days later. "I don't want any crowing or boasting," Mr Goodhew said, waving the sheets of paper in his hand.

"Or sobbing!" teased Cherry.

Mr Goodhew distributed the sheets round the class, then hurried back to his desk to watch them covertly. Katherine and Simon and Cherry looked a little smug, he saw, and Juliet and Anthony mightily relieved. Finley's face was expressionless – so empty of any emotion, Mr Goodhew thought, that the boy might just as well have been holding the list of his results upside down. But maybe there wasn't much to be either pleased or displeased about. He had, after all, acquitted himself fairly adequately. Not a disaster. It was, as Mr Goodhew had seen that morning, a rather boring line of Bs from top to bottom. The only mark that hadn't been a B was the mark that Miss Ellerman had given him for Physical Education (General). It had, as Mr Goodhew knew, been a harsh D until Mrs Harris had persuaded her colleague to soften it up to a C.

So. Not a good report. And not a bad one. (Just as Luke had said.)

Off the wall

Exactly one week before the end of term, Finley fell off the wall. It wasn't anybody's fault. Jeremy had booted the ball to Jamie, and Jamie had booted it as hard as he could. He had been aiming it towards Ygor, on the far side of the recreation ground, but didn't get the shot right. The ball hit Finley fair and square in the chest, and knocked him off the wall backwards.

Finley fell on his head.

Everyone scrambled over the wall, trying to help. Stuart and Cherry ran off to find a teacher. Tansy stood over Finley, telling everybody that it was important not to touch him. "He might have broken something."

"I could take off my shirt and slide it under his head," suggested Simon.

"Better not," Tansy said. "But you could lay it on top

of him, to keep him warm."

"Oh, come on, Tansy," said Alicia. "It's boiling hot today. He doesn't need stuff piling on top of him. He just needs to lie there quietly till he comes round."

"*If* he comes round," Jeremy muttered gloomily. "Poor Jamie might have accidentally killed him."

"Shut up!" said Juliet fiercely. "Shut up! Shut up! Shut up!"

Everyone, not just Jeremy, shut up and waited for a member of staff to come. It didn't take more than another minute. Miss Ellerman and Mr Chapman got there first by opening the fire doors that led out onto the neglected square of the abandoned car park on the far side of the wall.

"Is he stirring?" Miss Ellerman gently raised one of Finley's eyelids to peer at his pupils. "Hopefully, he's only been knocked out for a very short while."

Ms Leroy ran towards the huddle gathered round the boy. "Mr Porter has phoned for an ambulance."

"I think he's coming round," said Miss Ellerman. "Yes, look. He definitely seems to be stirring."

Everyone held their breath while Finley groaned.

"He's still to go to hospital," declared Miss Ellerman. "With head things, it's impossible to be too careful." She turned to everyone round her. "I want you all away from here," she said. "Give the poor boy some air. I want you all to go back over the wall, where you're supposed to be."

Some of them took a bit more persuasion than others. But by the time the paramedics arrived, everyone had been herded back over, into the recreation ground. The taller ones reported what they could see as Finley was lifted onto a stretcher and carried off.

"Will he die?" asked Jia Li.

"Of course not," Simon Parsons told her irritably. "He'll just have concussion. And a terrible headache when he wakes up."

"He did sort of wake up," said Anthony, "because if he'd still been dead unconscious, then he wouldn't have been groaning."

"How do you know?" asked Jia Li.

"I just do," said Anthony. And the three of them were still arguing about the matter when the buzzer rang to call them in to afternoon school.

Letting them talk

The notion that Finley might have been badly hurt consumed the class all afternoon. They couldn't settle at all. In the end, since it was in any case so near to the end of term, Mr Goodhew gave up on trying to get them to concentrate, cut short the lesson on electrolysis he'd planned, and let them talk.

"Will Finley come in tomorrow?" Akeem asked. "Or will he stay away until the holidays start?"

"I don't know, do I?" Mr Goodhew said. "I'm not a doctor. Or a soothsayer."

"Poor Finley," Tory said. "It was a long way to fall. Especially backwards. I bet it really, really hurt his head."

"He wouldn't even have felt it," Emma argued. "He was out cold."

"It must have been a real bang. He won't be sitting on that wall for quite a while."

"He won't be sitting on that wall again *at all*," said Mr Goodhew. "Mrs Harris has already had a word with Miss Willis about it, and she'll be putting that wall right out of bounds as from tomorrow."

They were appalled. "What, even for *Finley*?"

"What will he *do*?"

"Where will he *go*?"

"*Poor* Finley."

They all sat thinking for a moment about Finley. Alicia was the first to break the silence. "It was Finley who taught me how to tie my shoe laces," she remembered fondly. "Way back in primary school."

"He taught me how to keep my temper," Akeem said. Then, when he heard the sniggering around him, he added, "Well, *almost* keep it. Most of the time."

Katherine was not to be left out. "He taught me how to do optimal choice theory."

Everyone stared, including Mr Goodhew. So Katherine explained. "What I mean is, he told me that I could fiddle the hobbies timetable around to get things working better. So I did."

"He taught me how to tell people when I don't want to see a scary film," said Juliet. "Or have a party."

"Mrs Lapinska told her sister that Finley taught us all to stand still and look at a painting properly," Ygor told them.

"How on earth do you know that?" Mr Goodhew asked him.

"I heard her," Ygor said. "She told her sister in Russian, but I'm from Belarus, so I knew what she was saying."

"He taught me how to borrow properly," Stuart admitted.

They were all mystified. "Borrow *properly*? How do you borrow *properly*?"

"In maths," said Stuart.

"Oh, maths! I thought you meant in *borrowing*."

"I did."

Mr Goodhew cut short that argument. "Well, all of you clearly really do appreciate Finley as a class mate. So why don't you spend the last ten minutes of the lesson writing him Get Well messages."

"Can we just draw a picture?" Emma asked.

"Anything," said Mr Goodhew. "Just something nice and cheering."

"Will someone take them to him in the hospital?"

"If Finley is still in the hospital tomorrow," Mr Goodhew said, "I'll take them in to him myself."

God forbid!

There was no need. Early next morning, Miss Willis stopped Mr Goodhew in the corridor to tell him that Mrs Tandy had rung the school. She'd left the message that Finley had only been kept in hospital overnight because they were being so careful. All of the scans had come out fine, and he was fully awake and perfectly cheerful. "Almost himself again. He'll be back home today." So Mr Goodhew swept all the Get Well messages and pictures into a plastic bag and shoved them under his desk, out of the way.

But Finley's empty seat excited comment. Cherry began the conversation. "If Finley dies – "

Mr Goodhew stepped in at once. "There is no way that Finley's going to die. He's fine. He's even going to go back home today."

"All right," said Cherry, somewhat irritably. "But suppose that Finley *had* died – "

"Stop it!" said Mr Goodhew. "You are being ghoulish."

"I'm not," said Cherry. "I am simply trying to ask a question."

Jamie came to the support of his sister. "Cherry's allowed to ask *questions*."

Mr Goodhew gave Cherry a darkly warning look before he said, "Very well, Cherry. Ask me your question."

Cherry was not abashed. "If Finley had died," she said, "would you have gone to his funeral?"

For just a moment, Mr Goodhew was too disconcerted to answer. Then, "Yes, I would," he said. "And so would pretty well everyone else who ever knew him. And Miss Willis and I would have arranged it so that any of you who wanted to come with us would be welcome. And we would do the same for any one of you if – God forbid! – anything so horrible and unhappy should happen to you. And that is the end of my answer, Cherry, and it is also the end of this entire discussion. I do not want to hear another *word*."

And he so obviously meant it that even Cherry didn't try to argue or prolong the matter.

Only three more days

Finley showed up at lunch time the next day. "We're glad

to see you back," said Mr Goodhew. "I have a heap of Get Well notes and stuff for you here, under my desk."

"Not sure I need them," Finley admitted. "I'm perfectly all right."

"How was hospital?" Jeremy asked him.

"You're not allowed to get much sleep," said Finley. "Somebody comes along and shines a bright light in your eyes every five minutes to wake you up."

"To check your pupils," Mr Goodhew corrected him. "To make sure you're not falling into a coma."

"Well, I wasn't," Finley argued, somewhat irritably for him. "I was *asleep*."

"I meant, to make sure you'd be fully conscious if you were *awake*," explained Mr Goodhew.

"Well, I wasn't," Finley said again. "I was *asleep*."

The conversation seemed to be going nowhere, so Mr Goodhew moved to another topic. "Well, I should tell you, Finley, that there is a new school rule that's going to affect you more than anybody else. There will be no more sitting on that wall."

Clearly the class were still determined to object on Finley's behalf. "I'm sure Miss Willis isn't allowed to just make a new rule like this whenever she feels like it," Cherry said.

"Not in the middle of term time," Akeem insisted.

"Hardly the *middle* of term time," Katherine couldn't help correcting him.

Akeem amended his complaint, but only by a little. "Well, out of the blue."

Mr Goodhew felt obliged to put them right. "She is the head teacher, so I'm afraid she does. Mrs Harris has insisted on it, and Miss Willis has agreed."

Juliet turned in her chair to stare at Finley. She had, thought Mr Goodhew, gone a little pale. Hoping to soften the blow as much for Juliet as for Finley, he reminded her, "There's still the bench under the staffroom window. Finley can still sit on the bench."

"It's not the same, though, is it?" Jamie argued. And quite a few of them pitched in quite loudly to agree that it wasn't the same.

Jia Li tried to pour oil on troubled waters, "But there are only three more school days anyway. Then it's the holidays."

"Really?" said Finley. He sounded somewhat startled

by the news. And then, to Juliet's great relief, he smiled.

Who's getting Finley?

Mr Goodhew went into the staffroom with only one question in his mind. "Who's getting Finley next year?"

It seemed that no one had yet seen the lists, and most of the staff whom Mr Goodhew asked weren't even sure whose job it was to split them into their new classes.

"Isn't that Mrs Harris? Doesn't she usually do it?"

"I thought it was Dr Yates."

"Perhaps it's not decided yet. Perhaps it's something usually done over the summer break."

"But I need to know," said Mr Goodhew. "And I need to know now."

"Why?" Mrs Batterjee teased. "So you can worry about that Tandy boy all through the holidays?"

"It isn't funny," Mr Goodhew said. "He's a strange child. He takes a good bit of – "

He broke off. A good bit of what? What would the right word be? Understanding? Or patience, maybe?

"Decoding?" suggested Dr Rutter. "And if it's *that* he

needs, make sure they don't give him to me. I'm hopeless with the weird ones."

"We do try very hard not to use that word in this school," Mrs Hilliard reproved Dr Rutter, and not for the first time. But as the buzzer rang just at the moment she began to speak, he probably didn't hear her.

Singing

Juliet sat on the back step. She'd been helping her dad peg sheets on the line when his phone rang. He was behind her in the kitchen now, explaining something to a client while she sat waiting for him to come back, so they could finish the job.

The sheets they had already hung were billowing in the light wind, and Juliet was thinking about a song she'd learned in primary school. It was a sea shanty about unfurling sails, and setting off for new horizons. It was the first time that she'd come across the word horizon, she remembered.

Her dad came out again. "Stirring stuff," he said, grinning. "Something you're playing in Brass Band?"

"What?"

"What you were singing."

"Was I singing? Out *loud*?" Horrified, Juliet glanced to left and right to check there were no neighbours in their own gardens who might have overheard her.

Her father gave her a broad smile. "Yes," he said. "Singing your little heart out. Yes, you were."

No tinkering

Early next morning, forsaking his home class, Mr Goodhew went off in search of Mrs Harris. He found her hidden in an alcove halfway along the music corridor, frowning at a fistful of print-outs.

"Is that the class lists for next year?" he asked her. "May I take a peek?"

Mrs Harris sighed gently. "I have already done it."

"What?"

"Separated your twins."

"Jamie and Cherry? Well, good. I'm sure Jamie will blossom away from his somewhat overbearing sister. But the one I'm worried about right now is Finley Tandy. I don't want him going to Dr Rutter." After a moment, he added, as a clincher, "And I know for a fact that Dr Rutter doesn't want him."

"How did he do in the exams?"

"Middling," admitted Mr Goodhew. "Not all that good, but not at all bad, either."

"Well, if he's only middling, I very much doubt if I'll have put him in with Gordon Rutter," Mrs Harris said. While Mr Goodhew stood beside her on tenterhooks, trying not to loom, she shuffled through her print-outs. "Okay, so that's Gordon's lot. No Tandy there. And here's Miss Clement's new class. No. Not there either. Oh, look! It's me who has him next year. I've put him down as one of mine."

"That's fine, then," Mr Goodhew said, immensely relieved. He set off back towards his class, only to spin round again.

"You won't let anyone change that, will you, Doris? You won't let anyone tinker with your list?"

"We do quite often have a few last minute changes, Julian. You know that."

"Well, don't let Finley Tandy slip through your

fingers," Mr Goodhew warned her sternly. "Not without speaking to me. He has to come to you."

Mrs Harris couldn't help smiling. "I must say, Julian, you do take a very great deal of trouble over a boy who *is* supposedly no trouble."

"Do I?" Mr Goodhew was startled to hear it put so bluntly. "I suppose I do."

Done deal!

Finley caught up with Juliet at the corner of the road. He tapped her on the shoulder and she turned, startled, telling him, "You don't come home this way."

"No," he said. "I just came after you. I want to tell you something."

"What?"

"I don't want you worrying about me," Finley said. "I know how you worry."

"I'm getting a whole lot better at not worrying," Juliet told him. "Surina says so."

"Surina?"

Juliet realised she was going to have to explain. "She's

the person I have to go to see every few weeks. Because of the panic attacks." But something had happened on the last visit that Juliet was so proud of, she suddenly wanted to tell someone about it. Who better than Finley? "And Surina says I'm almost ready to fly. She says that from now on she only wants me to clock in every three months or so, and even if I want to do that just with a phone call, that will probably be fine."

"That's really good," said Finley kindly. "Well done, you."

The two of them stood side by side, both looking at the pavement and saying nothing more for a short while. Then Juliet asked, "So what did you want to tell me?"

Finley shrugged. "Just what I said really. That you mustn't worry about me. You see, the wall isn't nearly as important as you think."

"Isn't it? You're always up there, after all. Almost the whole of every break and lunch hour."

Finley waved a hand somewhat airily, as if to brush the weight of this observation aside. "Yes. I really like it up there. But it doesn't *matter*."

"Why not?"

Finley shrugged. "It's a bit hard to explain. But mostly it's because I just don't work like that. I don't feel what I feel because of where I am. It doesn't work that way."

Juliet gave this some thought. And it was true that Finley did always seem to be the way he was wherever he was sitting. Or standing. Or simply being. Hadn't she watched him all year, covertly admiring this very air of calm he wore around him like a see-through cloak? She'd even tried to copy him a little when things were worrying her. More than once, when she was fretting, she'd looked across at Finley, and simply seeing him there had made it easier for her to breathe the way Surina had taught her, slowly and calmly, until her heart stopped thumping and the horrid pictures in her head had gone away.

"So you won't mind?" she said. "You'll just be happy on the bench?"

"Not sure about the bench," he said. "It's not exactly in the best place, is it?"

"What, right there underneath the staffroom window? I suppose not." Then Juliet had an idea. "But we can move it." The moment she suggested it, she knew it was the thing to do. "We'll budge it just a tiny bit every day. No one will notice. And if anyone does, all that they'll think is that Mr Harley shifted it for some reason of his own. No one will care."

Finley was smiling. "Yes. We'll do that. We'll start on the first day back."

Juliet laughed. "By half term, we could have it halfway round the side." She gave him one last eager look. "And you'll be happy till then?"

"Listen," said Finley. "You have to understand. I'm sort of happy anywhere. It's just the way I am."

"So I'm not to worry about you?" Juliet found herself testing the idea in her head. "And in return, will you not worry about me?"

"Sure," Finley promised.

Juliet stuck out her hand. "Done deal." she said. (It was what Clare and Cassie always said when they agreed on something.)

Finley stuck out his own. "Done deal," he agreed.

Then he turned round to go back home his own way.

No flies on me

A man with a clipboard and notebook arrived the following morning in the middle of break. Accompanied by Mr Goodhew, he strolled along the side of the wall, then stepped out further into the recreation ground to take a few photos.

Cherry showed up at Mr Goodhew's side, practically under his arm, startling him somewhat. "Who's that?" she asked, pointing at the man taking photos. "And why is he here, Mr Goodhew?"

"I've no idea," said Mr Goodhew. "I was just asked to bring him out here and stay with him till he's done."

Akeem materialised now on Mr Goodhew's other side. "What, to protect us in case he's a psychopathic child killer?"

Unruffled, Mr Goodhew answered, "More likely to protect the man from you lot."

"Look, he's measuring," said Cherry. "I know exactly what he's doing. He's measuring the wall to see how many skips he'll need to get rid of all the rubble. I bet Miss Willis has just hired his firm to take it down."

"No flies on you, are there, Cherry?" said Mr Goodhew. "I wouldn't want to be the town councillor who gets on the wrong side of you when you grow up." Then he remembered Cherry and Jamie's mother was the local mayor, and turned to apologise. But Cherry was already dancing away, singing at the top of her voice, "No flies on me! No flies on me! Oh, no. No flies on me!"

No one expecting to be kidnapped?

On the very last morning, Mr Goodhew finished registration, then looked round the class and demanded, "Anyone feeling sick today?"

Nobody claimed that they were feeling sick.

"Anyone planning to slope off and play hooky?"

No one admitted this, either.

"And there is no one here expecting to be kidnapped before I take the register one last time this afternoon?"

All of them stared at him blankly.

"Right, then," he said. "As I'll be quite busy today, I'm going to read out the names right now of all the

218

people who'll get certificates for Perfect Attendance." He turned to Finley. "You're most unlucky," he told him. "You just missed getting on the list because of falling off the wall."

"That's all right," Finley said. "I've got a heap of them at home from Janson Road."

Mr Goodhew read out the list. It was a fair few of the class, and Juliet was sure she heard her name. But maybe it was just a big mistake. She'd missed so many days at her old school before they'd finally sent her off to talk to Surina. She couldn't remember being off for any colds or headaches. Still, it would be very strange if she'd not missed a single day this whole school year.

So Juliet waited till the buzzer rang and Mr Goodhew sent them off, then stayed behind just long enough to ask him, "Was I really one of them? Really?"

Mr Goodhew could tell she couldn't quite believe it so he opened up the register again, and showed her. "Here you are. Juliet Walker. You make it through today and you will have one hundred per cent attendance. Well done you!"

He left her standing there, half-dazed with

astonishment, thinking first, 'Well done me!', then thinking how very pleased and proud her dad and Amanda were both going to be.

Goodbye Wall

At the start of the afternoon session, Mr Goodhew made an announcement. "I want everyone packed up and ready to go home five minutes before the last buzzer goes."

"Are you letting us out early? Ace stuff!"

"If I run, I might be able to get the early bus."

"I'll still have to hang around until my nan gets here to pick me up."

Mr Goodhew felt obliged to dampen their enthusiasm. "You're not getting out early, I'm afraid. It's just that there is something we must do."

"What?" Cherry demanded.

"You wait and see. It will only take a couple of minutes."

"*Nothing* that happens in a school just takes a couple of minutes," Cherry reminded him. "You're *always* telling us that. We'll probably end up getting out later than everyone else. And it's the last day of term!"

"What do you want us to do anyway?" demanded Terence.

Some others backed him up. "Why can't you tell us now?"

Mr Goodhew ignored the pleas, simply repeating, "Just make sure you're all ready."

And sure enough, more than five minutes before the last buzzer was due to sound, they were all at their desks behind untidy mounds of bulging book bags, sporting gear, peculiar leftover art works, musical instruments and all the odd footwear and clothing unearthed on Miss Ellerman's last trawl of the changing rooms and cloakrooms.

"Leave all that where it is," said Mr Goodhew. "We're going out."

Baffled, they followed him along the corridor and out of the south door, into the recreation area.

"Spread out," said Mr Goodhew. "Don't just stand there in clumps. Spread out and say goodbye to the wall."

"Really?"

"Say goodbye to a *wall*?"

Cherry sounded ecstatic. "I knew it! I was right! They're taking the wall down over the holidays! It won't be here at all when we get back."

"What will it look like?" Stuart asked.

"Just not there any more," said Tansy.

"We'll have a lot more room," said Jamie. "Now we'll be able to play footie right up as far as the back doors."

"What was the wall built there for, anyway?" asked Emma. "It isn't doing anything except keeping us out of the bit behind it."

"Unless you fall off it," said Simon, grinning at Finley.

" That was the old staff car park," Mr Goodhew said. "So the wall served a useful purpose in its time. But now it's going, so I wanted you to have the chance to say goodbye to it."

Cherry grinned. "No, you didn't, Mr Goodhew. You wanted *Finley* to be able to say goodbye to it, because it's sort of his wall."

Mr Goodhew hoped very much that his discomfiture

wasn't showing. He feared his face might even be going red as he insisted, "Well, whoever wants to, really."

But Finley saved the day. Stepping forward, he lay both hands flat on the wall and told it solemnly, "Goodbye then, Wall."

Partly from sympathy, but mostly for a laugh, most of them followed his example. "Goodbye, Old Wall."

"Farewell, Wall."

"Ta-ra, Wall. You've been a very good friend."

"So sad to see you go."

"Tragic."

Then it turned silly.

"Poor wall! To stand here for so many years and then, *poof!*, to be gone!"

"Oh, dearest Wall. I shan't sleep for weeping. Every morning I shall have to peg up my pillowcase to dry, ready to weep again."

"All right, all right," said Mr Goodhew. "That's enough." Mercifully, the sound of the very last buzzer of the school year echoed across the recreation ground. "Off you go. Back to the classroom and don't leave any of your stuff lying about to annoy the cleaners. I don't want to come across so much as a chewed pencil stub. Take everything home – *everything*. Have a really good time, don't do anything too silly while we're not watching you, and don't forget to come back after the holidays."

Few of them heard to the very end of this, his termly valediction. They were all rushing back towards the south door. All except Finley.

"Well," Mr Goodhew asked him, "Are you going to be all right?"

Finley looked up. "All right?"

"I suppose," Mr Goodhew explained, still a little embarrassed, "you have spent an awful lot of happy hours up on this wall. That bench will not be quite the same."

"No," Finley agreed. "The bench won't be the same. But I did tell you I was happy anywhere."

And Mr Goodhew suddenly remembered that that was, indeed, what Finley had said to him back on that very first day of the first term: "Oh, I'll be happy. I'm happy absolutely everywhere. And all the time."

"That's good," he said.

The two of them gave Finley's wall one last long look, then turned together to walk back towards the school. Neither of them had any more to say. At the south door, Finley took off to fetch his school bag and his sports gear before walking home. And Mr Goodhew walked along to the staffroom to fetch the first of several boxes he still had to pack into the back of his car.

Hurry up, Jools!

Juliet put down her school bag and sports bag and tennis racket and bulky drawing pad and two oversized binders and waited for her dad to drive around the corner. Both of them had known that she'd have far too much to carry, and he had promised her that he would leave work early to pick her up in the car.

The minutes passed. Had he forgotten her?

No, here was a car she recognised, just pulling in onto the strictly forbidden area of painted zig-zag lines beside the crossing. And that was Cassie, halfway out of the window, yelling, "Hurry up, Jools! Mum says she'll get a ticket!"

Juliet gathered up her stuff and clumsily ran with some of it banging painfully against her legs until she reached the car. Cassie had already pushed the door open, and the moment that she had taken in half of the stuff and Juliet was safely strapped in beside Clare with the rest, Amanda pulled the car back out onto the road again.

"Sorry about the change of plan," said Amanda. "Your dad got an important client in at the last minute and asked if I could come to fetch you instead. We're going back to our place."

"But only for an hour or so," said Clare. "And after that, we're going to meet your dad at *Bella Italia*."

"End of term treat," said Amanda.

"Lovely," said Juliet. And while the other two were busy teasing one another about a boy who'd waved at Clare, but not at Cassie, Juliet sat thinking. No one except her mother had ever called her 'Jools', and even then her dad had always ticked her off for doing it. "Why give a child a beautiful name, only to ruin it?"

The name had sounded very strange, coming again after so long, and from somebody else.

But in the end, Juliet decided that she didn't mind at all. It made her feel as if, now, she had become a real part of their family, and she liked that.

Finley goes home

Finley sat with his back against the school fence, his stuff piled round him. He'd been there for quite a while already, and he was wondering if Luke had forgotten that he had promised to meet him to help him carry his gear home. Surreptitiously Finley fished out his phone, before remembering that, firstly, he was off school grounds, and secondly, the term was finished. No need to hide it any more.

There was a message from his brother. *On the way.*

So Finley sat peaceably. He had been counting how many of those passing by as they spilled out of the gates still called him what Mr Goodhew had once referred to as 'the full Finley', and how many of them over the past school year had casually shortened his name. It seemed to him that, somehow without doing anything at all himself, he might be gradually turning into a Finn.

He was looking in quite the wrong direction when his brother finally came around the corner.

"Where's Turfy?"

"At home," Luke explained. "I had a driving lesson, and didn't fancy having him drool down my neck. Mrs Patil's just dropped me off but there were roadworks beyond the roundabout. That's why I'm late." He reached down and swung Finley's bulging backpack onto his shoulder, then picked up the heavy sports bag. "You take the saxophone," he ordered. "And the music folder, and tennis racquet and whatever is in that funny shaped bag there."

"That's cooking gear," said Finley. "And a felt mouse. Or gerbil." He sighed. "I wish I was as tall as you."

"You will be one day," Luke assured him. "Taller, in fact."

"How do you know?"

"Mum says," said Luke. "Something about you being measured when you're born. They sort of *know*."

"Truly?"

"Unless you don't get fed properly along the way," said Luke. "Speaking of which, Mum's taking us to *Bella*

Italia tonight. End of term treat."

"I've earned it," Finley said. "It's been a really, really long year."

"Only six more to go," said Luke.

And if Finley hadn't been hampered by the saxophone, the music case, the tennis racquet and the funny-shaped bag of cooking gear and a felt mouse (or gerbil), he would have pushed his brother. Hard.

No one. Just a friend.

Juliet was settled with the rest of the family in one of the bigger booths of the restaurant. She had Clare on one side and Cassie on the other, facing her dad and Amanda. The five of them had already given their orders when Finley and his mum and brother came through the door.

"Hi, Juliet," said Finley as the three of them walked past, following the boy who was showing them to their own table.

"Hi, Finley," Juliet said.

Cassie was on it like a flash. "Who's that? That boy

who said hello to you. Who is he?"

"No one," said Juliet. "Just Finley. Just a friend."

She caught her father's eye, and saw that he was looking very proud of her, and she felt wonderful. Wonderful.

*

At the far end of the restaurant, Luke waited till the three of them were seated before he asked his brother, "So who was that?"

"Who?" Finley said.

"That girl you said hello to just this minute. Back there."

"Oh," Finley said. "No one. Just Juliet. Just a friend."

Luke smiled. But when Finley's mother kicked his ankle sharply under the table, he didn't go on to try to tease his brother. He just dropped his head, like Finley, and began to study the menu.

And everything looked good.

Afterword

In his very first exchange with his new teacher, Finley makes his own state of mind perfectly clear. "Oh, I'll be happy," he says. "I'm happy absolutely everywhere. And all the time." You will probably already know that happiness is not always easy to grasp. Or keep.

Juliet is nowhere near as lucky as Finley. She's a worrier. We soon learn the reasons for the anxieties she feels and her loss of confidence in the world around her. So it is cheering to see her getting more and more of a grip, and a returning sense of her own capabilities as we go through the story. Surina, her counsellor, is obviously helping. But so too – perhaps even more so, and without knowing it – is Finley.

Finley is what adults often call 'his own person'. He doesn't seek to be different. He has the rare and enviable gift of just accepting himself. It's hard to imagine someone like Finley even bothering to look at social media. (I'm the author, and even I was astonished, to find out, right at the end of the book, that Finley carried a mobile phone.) It's quite impossible to see him taking any interest in what other people think of him, except perhaps, if that turned out to be nasty, to wonder mildly what in their own lives had made them want to say something so mean or aggressive about somebody else.

Finley is at peace with himself. Even on the occasion when three separate teachers have as good as told him he should buck up a bit about his work, he comes to the conclusion that, like his beloved dog Turfy, there's hardly any point in trying to be different.

Parent and teachers, of course, are always hoping for a little bit more. Naturally they want you, as they so often put it, to 'be the best that you can be'. Maybe work a bit harder for exams, practice your flute more often, improve at your chosen sports. You might even catch them hinting that they wish you could do something that seems halfway to impossible, like 'make more friends'.

This can, for some people at some times, turn a bit sour. Why can't they be satisfied with you just the way you come? But there is a middle way between striving endlessly and simply coasting along, and it's important to try to find it.

Very few people can just be happy in the way that Finley can. But there are tried and tested methods for altering your own moods and defeating your worries. Music's a good mood changer. (Just don't pick the gloomiest artist you know.) One child I know is a dreadful worrier and her mum always asks her, "Can you remember what you were fretting about this time last year, Emma?" Of course she never can, and that tends to put her current worry into proportion.

And that's the root of it. Keeping a sense of proportion. Working out what the very worst that can happen is, and reminding yourself that loads of people have got over even that. (And, believe me, whatever it is, they have.) I read the daily papers and feel so gloomy. Then I read my own local paper, about my own community, and it is full of good cheer, charitable works and well-lived lives. You really mustn't take on all the worries of the wider world until you're grown and ready.

Way, way back, when I myself was young, we all had something called Desiderata on our bedroom walls. A poet called Max Ehrmann wrote it in 1927. It started, *'Go placidly amid the noise and haste, and remember what peace there may be in silence.'* And it ended, *'With all its sham, drudgery and broken dreams, it is still a beautiful world. Be cheerful. Strive to be happy.'*

You won't find better advice anywhere.

Also by Anne Fine and available from Old Barn Books:

A *The Times* and *The Sunday Times* Book of the Week

'A brilliantly rewarding read' – LoveReading

Accompanying his engineer father on a work trip,
Louie is stranded by an earthquake in an isolated world
peopled by ghostly figures. Overwhelmed by the misery
of the silent Endlanders and grieving the loss of his own
brother, Louie realises there is something he can do to
help them all face the future again. But will he find
the courage to do it?

ISBN: 9781910646823

About the Author

Former Children's Laureate Anne Fine has written over seventy books for children and won many prizes and accolades, including twice winning the Carnegie Medal. She began to write after the birth of her first child, when she was unable to get to the library to change her books in a snowstorm, and she hasn't stopped since. Her writing very often tackles series social issues (Anne studied Politics and History at university) but can also be laugh-out-loud funny and her range is demonstrated by the successes of *Madam Doubtfire* and *Goggle Eyes*.

Ms Fine has often been described as 'outspoken' but in *On The Wall* she explores how we can all benefit from a little peace and quiet: something she learned to treasure as a child, growing up in a small house with four siblings.